William T. Dobson

Poetical Ingenuities and Eccentricities

William T. Dobson

Poetical Ingenuities and Eccentricities

ISBN/EAN: 9783337406257

Printed in Europe, USA, Canada, Australia, Japan

Cover: Foto ©Andreas Hilbeck / pixelio.de

More available books at **www.hansebooks.com**

POETICAL INGENUITIES

AND ECCENTRICITIES.

POETICAL INGENUITIES

AND

ECCENTRICITIES

SELECTED AND EDITED BY

WILLIAM T. DOBSON

AUTHOR OF "LITERARY FRIVOLITIES," ETC.

London

CHATTO AND WINDUS, PICCADILLY

1882

PREFACE.

THE favourable reception of "Literary Frivolities" by the Press has led to the preparation of this work as a Sequel, in which the only sin so far charged against the "Frivolities"— that of omission—will be found fully atoned for.

Those curious in regard to the historical and literary accounts of several of the various phases of composition exemplified in this work, will find these fully enough noticed in "Literary Frivolities," in which none of the examples were strictly original, and had been gathered from many outlying corners of the world of literature. In the present work, however, will be found a number of pieces which have not hitherto been "glorified in type," and these have been furnished by various literary gentlemen, among whom may be named Professor

E. H. Palmer and J. Appleton Morgan, LL.D., of New York. Assistance in "things both new and old" has also been given by Charles G. Leland, Esq. (Hans Breitmann), W. Bence Jones, Esq., J. F. Huntingdon, Esq. (Cambridge, U.S.); whilst particular thanks are due to Mr. Lewis Carroll for a kindly and courteous permission to quote from his works.

With regard to a few of the extracts, the difficulty of finding their authors has been a bar to requesting permission to use them; but in every case endeavour has been made to acknowledge the source whence they are derived.

CONTENTS.

POETICAL INGENUITIES

AND

ECCENTRICITIES.

THE PARODY.

ARODY is the name generally given to a humorous or burlesque imitation of a serious poem or song, of which it so far preserves the style and words of the original as that the latter may be easily recognised; it also may be said to consist in the application of high-sounding poetry to familiar objects, should be confined within narrow limits, and only adapted to light and momentary occasions. Though by no means the highest kind of literary composition, and generally used to ridicule the poets, still many might think their reputation increased rather than diminished by the involuntary applause of imitators and parodists, and have no objection that their

works afford the public double amusement—first
in the original, and afterwards in the travesty,
though the parodist may not always be intel-
lectually up to the level of his prototype. Parodies
are best, however, when short and striking—when
they produce mirth by the happy imitation of some
popular passage, or when they mix instruction with
amusement, by showing up some latent absurdity
or developing the disguises of bad taste.

The invention of this humoristic style of composition has been attributed to the Greeks, from whose
language the name itself is derived (*para*, beside ;
ode, a song) ; the first to use it being supposed to
be Hegemon of Thasos, who flourished during the
Peloponnesian War ; by others the credit of the
invention is given to Hipponax, who in his picture
of a glutton, parodies Homer's description of the
feats of Achilles in fighting with his hero in eating.
This work begins as follows :

" Sing, O celestial goddess, Eurymedon, foremost of
    gluttons,
  Whose stomach devours like Charybdis, eater un-
    matched among mortals."

The Battle of the Frogs and Mice (The " Batra-
chomyomachia"), also a happy specimen of the
parody is said to be a travesty of Homer's

"Iliad," and numerous examples will be found in the comedies of Aristophanes. Among the Romans this form of literary composition made its appearance at the period of the Decline, and all the power of Nero could not prevent Persius from parodying his verses. The French among modern nations have been much given to it, whilst in the English language there are many examples, one of the earliest being the parodying of Milton by John Philips, one of the most artificial poets of his age (1676–1708). He was an avowed imitator of Milton, and certainly evinced considerable talent in his peculiar line. Philips wrote in blank verse a poem on the victory of Blenheim, and another on Cider, the latter in imitation of the Georgics. His best work, however, is that from which there follows a quotation, a parody on "Paradise Lost," considered by Steele to be the best burlesque poem extant.

THE SPLENDID SHILLING.

> "'Sing, heavenly muse!
> Things unattempted yet, in prose or rhyme,'
> A shilling, breeches, and chimeras dire.

Happy the man, who, void of care and strife,
In silken or in leathern purse retains
A Splendid Shilling : he nor hears with pain
New oysters cried, nor sighs for cheerful ale ;

But with his friends, when nightly mists arise,
To Juniper's *Magpie*, or *Town-hall* * repairs :
Where, mindful of the nymph, whose wanton eye
Transfixed his soul, and kindled amorous flames,
Chloe or Phillis, he each circling glass
Wishes her health, and joy, and equal love.
Meanwhile he smokes, and laughs at merry tale,
Or pun ambiguous, or conundrum quaint.
But I, whom griping penury surrounds,
And hunger, sure attendant upon want,
With scanty offals, and small acid tiff,
Wretched repast ! my meagre corpse sustain :
Then solitary walk, or doze at home
In garret vile, and with a warning puff
Regale chilled fingers ; or from tube as black
As winter chimney, or well-polished jet,
Exhale mundungus, ill-perfuming scent :
Not blacker tube, nor of a shorter size,
Smokes Cambro-Briton (versed in pedigree,
Sprung from Cadwallader and Arthur, kings
Full famous in romantic tale) when he
O'er many a craggy hill and barren cliff,
Upon a cargo of famed Cestrian cheese,
High over-shadowing rides, with a design
To vend his wares, or at th' Avonian mart,
Or Maridunum, or the ancient town
Yclep'd Brechinia, or where Vaga's stream
Encircles Ariconium, fruitful soil !

* Two well-known alehouses in Oxford, about 1700.

Whence flows nectareous wines, that well may vie
With Massic, Setin, or renowned Falern.
  Thus, while my joyless minutes tedious flow
With looks demur, and silent pace, a dun,
Horrible monster ! hated by gods and men,
To my aërial citadel ascends :
With vocal heel thrice thundering at my gate ;
With hideous accent thrice he calls ; I know
The voice ill-boding, and the solemn sound.
What should I do ?. or whither turn ? Amazed,
Confounded, to the dark recess I fly
Of wood-hole ; straight my bristling hairs erect
Through sudden fear : a chilly sweat bedews
My shuddering limbs, and (wonderful to tell !)
My tongue forgets her faculty of speech ;
So horrible he seems ! His faded brow
Intrenched with many a frown, and conic beard,
And spreading band, admired by modern saints,
Disastrous acts forebode ; in his right hand
Long scrolls of paper solemnly he waves,
With characters and figures dire inscribed,
Grievous to mortal eyes (ye gods, avert
Such plagues from righteous men !) Behind him
      stalks
Another monster, not unlike himself,
Sullen of aspect, by the vulgar called
A catchpoll, whose polluted hands the gods
With force incredible, and magic charms,
First have endued : if he his ample palm

Should haply on ill-fated shoulder lay
Of debtor, straight his body, to the touch
Obsequious (as whilom knights were wont),
To some enchanted castle is conveyed,
Where gates impregnable, and coercive chains
In durance strict detain him, till, in form
Of money, Pallas sets him free.

    Beware, ye debtors! when ye walk, beware,
Be circumspect; oft with insidious ken
This caitiff eyes your steps aloof, and oft
Lies perdue in a nook or gloomy cave,
Prompt to enchant some inadvertent wretch
With his unhallowed touch. So (poets sing)
Grimalkin, to domestic vermin sworn
An everlasting foe, with watchful eye
Lies nightly brooding o'er a chinky gap,
Portending her fell claws, to thoughtless mice
Sure ruin. So her disembowelled web
Arachne, in a hall or kitchen, spreads
Obvious to vagrant flies: she secret stands
Within her woven cell; the humming prey,
Regardless of their fate, rush on the toils
Inextricable; nor will aught avail
Their arts, or arms, or shapes of lovely hue:
The wasp insidious, and the buzzing drone,
And butterfly, proud of expanded wings
Distinct with gold, entangled in her snares,
Useless resistance make: with eager strides
She towering flies to her expected spoils:

Then, with envenomed jaws, the vital blood
Drinks of reluctant foes, and to her cave
Their bulky carcasses triumphant drags." . . . .

Perhaps the best English examples of the true parody—the above being more of an imitation—are to be found in the " Rejected Addresses " of the brothers James and Horace Smith. This work owed its origin to the reopening of Drury Lane Theatre in 1812, after its destruction by fire. The managers, in the true spirit of tradesmen, issued an advertisement calling for Addresses, one of which should be spoken on the opening night. Forty-three were sent in for competition. Overwhelmed by the amount of talent thus placed at their disposal, the managers summarily rejected the whole, and placed themselves under the care of Lord Byron, whose composition, after all, was thought by some to be, if not unworthy, at least ill-suited for the occasion. Mr. Ward, the secretary of the Theatre, having casually started the idea of publishing a series of " Rejected Addresses," composed by the most popular authors of the day, the brothers Smith eagerly adopted the suggestion, and in six weeks the volume was published, and received by the public with enthusiastic delight. They were principally humorous imitations of eminent authors, and Lord Jeffrey said of them in the *Edinburgh Review:* "I take them indeed to be the very best imitations (and often of difficult originals) that ever were made; and, considering their great extent and variety, to indicate a talent to which I do not know where to look for a parallel. Some few of them descend to the level of parodies; but by far the greater part are of a much higher description." The one which follows is in imitation of Crabbe, and was written by James Smith, and Jeffrey thought it "the best piece in the collection. It is an exquisite and masterly imitation, not only of the peculiar style, but of the taste, temper, and manner of description of that most original author." Crabbe himself said regarding it, that it "was admirably done."

The Theatre.

" 'Tis sweet to view, from half-past five to six.
Our long wax candles, with short cotton wicks,
Touched by the lamplighter's Promethean art,
Start into light, and make the lighter start;
To see red Phœbus through the gallery-pane
Tinge with his beam the beams of Drury Lane;
While gradual parties fill our widen'd pit,
And gape, and gaze, and wonder, ere they sit.

    At first, while vacant seats give choice and ease,
Distant or near, they settle where they please;

But when the multitude contracts the span,
And seats are rare, they settle where they can.
  Now the full benches to late-comers doom
No room for standing, miscalled *standing-room.*
  Hark ! the check-taker moody silence breaks,
And bawling ' Pit full ! ' gives the check he takes ;
Yet onward still the gathering numbers cram,
Contending crowders shout the frequent damn,
And all is bustle, squeeze, row, jabbering, and jam.

  See to their desks Apollo's sons repair—
Swift rides the rosin o'er the horse's hair !
In unison their various tones to tune,
Murmurs the hautboy, growls the hoarse bassoon ;
In soft vibration sighs the whispering lute,
Tang goes the harpsichord, too-too the flute,
Brays the loud trumpet, squeaks the fiddle sharp,
Winds the French horn, and twangs the tingling harp ;
Till, like great Jove, the leader, figuring in,
Attunes to order the chaotic din.
Now all seems hushed ; but no, one fiddle will
Give, half ashamed, a tiny flourish still.
Foiled in his crash, the leader of the clan
Reproves with frowns the dilatory man :
Then on his candlestick thrice taps his bow,
Nods a new signal, and away they go.
  Perchance, while pit and gallery cry ' Hats off ! '
And awed Consumption checks his chided cough,
Some giggling daughter of the Queen of Love
Drops, reft of pin, her play-bill from above ;

Like Icarus, while laughing galleries clap,
Soars, ducks, and dives in air the printed scrap;
But, wiser far than he, combustion fears,
And, as it flies, eludes the chandeliers;
Till, sinking gradual, with repeated twirl,
It settles, curling, on a fiddler's curl,
Who from his powdered pate the intruder strikes,
And, for mere malice, sticks it on the spikes.

Say, why these Babel strains from Babel tongues?
Who's that calls 'Silence!' with such leathern lungs!
He who, in quest of quiet, 'Silence!' hoots,
Is apt to make the hubbub he imputes.

What various swains our motley walls contain!—
Fashion from Moorfields, honour from Chick Lane;
Bankers from Paper Buildings here resort,
Bankrupts from Golden Square and Riches Court;
From the Haymarket canting rogues in grain,
Gulls from the Poultry, sots from Water Lane;
The lottery-cormorant, the auction shark,
The full-price master, and the half-price clerk;
Boys who long linger at the gallery-door,
With pence twice five—they want but twopence more;
Till some Samaritan the twopence spares,
And sends them jumping up the gallery-stairs.

Critics we boast who ne'er their malice balk,
But talk their minds—we wish they'd mind their talk;
Big-worded bullies, who by quarrels live—
Who give the lie, and tell the lie they give;
Jews from St. Mary Axe, for jobs so wary,
That for old clothes they'd even axe St. Mary;

And bucks with pockets empty as their pate,
Lax in their gaiters, laxer in their gait;
Who oft, when we our house lock up, carouse
With tippling tipstaves in a lock-up house.

    Yet here, as elsewhere, Chance can joy bestow
Where scowling fortune seem'd to threaten woe.

    John Richard William Alexander Dwyer
Was footman to Justinian Stubbs, Esquire;
But when John Dwyer listed in the Blues,
Emanuel Jennings polished Stubbs's shoes;
Emanuel Jennings brought his youngest boy
Up as a corn-cutter—a safe employ;
In Holywell Street, St. Pancras, he was bred
(At number twenty-seven, it is said),
Facing the pump, and near the Granby's head;
He would have bound him to some shop in town,
But with a premium he could not come down.
Pat was the urchin's name—a red-haired youth,
Fonder of purl and skittle-grounds than truth.

    Silence, ye gods! to keep your tongues in awe,
The Muse shall tell an accident she saw.

    Pat Jennings in the upper gallery sat,
But, leaning forward, Jennings lost his hat;
Down from the gallery the beaver flew,
And spurned the one to settle in the two.
How shall he act? Pay at the gallery-door
Two shillings for what cost, when new, but four?
Or till half-price, to save his shilling, wait,
And gain his hat again at half-past eight?

Now, while his fears anticipate a thief,
John Mullens whispered, 'Take my handkerchief.'
'Thank you,' cries Pat; 'but one won't make a line.'
'Take mine,' cried Wilson; and cried Stokes, 'Take
    mine.'
A motley cable soon Pat Jennings ties,
Where Spitalfields with real India vies.
Like Iris' bow down darts the painted clue,
Starred, striped, and spotted, yellow, red, and blue,
Old calico, torn silk, and muslin new.
George Green below, with palpitating hand,
Loops the last 'kerchief to the beaver's band—
Upsoars the prize ! The youth, with joy unfeigned,
Regained the felt, and felt what he regained ;
While to the applauding galleries grateful Pat
Made a low bow, and touched the ransomed hat !"

From the same work is taken this parody on a
beautiful passage in Southey's "Kehama :"

    "Midnight, yet not a nose
  From Tower Hill to Piccadilly snored !
    Midnight, yet not a nose
  From Indra drew the essence of repose.
    See with what crimson fury,
By Indra fann'd, the god of fire ascends the walls of
    Drury !
    The tops of houses, blue with lead,
    Bend beneath the landlord's tread ;

Master and 'prentice, serving man and lord,
    Nailor and tailor,
    Grazier and brazier,
  Through streets and alleys poured,
    All, all abroad to gaze,
    And wonder at the blaze.
Thick calf, fat foot, and slim knee,
Mounted on roof and chimney ;
The mighty roast, the mighty stew
     To see,
    As if the dismal view
Were but to them a mighty jubilee."

The brothers Smith reproduced Byron in the familiar "Childe Harold" stanza, both in style and thought :

" For what is Hamlet, but a hare in March ?
  And what is Brutus but a croaking owl ?
And what is Rolla ? Cupid steeped in starch,
  Orlando's helmet in Augustin's cowl.
Shakespeare, how true thine adage, 'fair is foul !'
  To him whose soul is with fruition fraught,
The song of Braham is an Irish howl,
  Thinking is but an idle waste of thought,
And nought is everything, and everything is nought."

Moore, also, was imitated in the same way, as in these verses :

"The apples that grew on the fruit-tree of knowledge
   By women were plucked, and she still wears the prize,
To tempt us in theatre, senate, or college—
   I mean the love-apples that bloom in the eyes.

There, too, is the lash which, all statutes controlling,
   Still governs the slaves that are made by the fair;
For man is the pupil who, while her eye's rolling,
   Is lifted to rapture or sunk in despair."

From the parody on Sir Walter Scott, it is difficult to select, being all good; calling from Scott
himself the remark, "I must have done this myself,
though I forget on what occasion."

A Tale of Drury Lane.

BY W. S.

"As Chaos which, by heavenly doom,
   Had slept in everlasting gloom,
   Started with terror and surprise,
   When light first flashed upon her eyes:
   So London's sons in nightcap woke,
      In bedgown woke her dames,
   For shouts were heard mid fire and smoke,
   And twice ten hundred voices spoke,
      'The playhouse is in flames.'
   And lo! where Catherine Street extends,
   A fiery tail its lustre lends
      To every window pane:

Blushes each spout in Martlet Court,
And Barbican, moth-eaten fort,
And Covent Garden kennels sport
　　A bright ensanguined drain ;
Meux's new brewhouse shows the light,
Rowland Hill's chapel, and the height
　　Where patent shot they sell :
The Tennis Court, so fair and tall,
Partakes the ray, with Surgeons' Hall,
The ticket porters' house of call,
Old Bedlam, close by London Wall,
Wright's shrimp and oyster shop withal,
　　And Richardson's hotel.
Nor these alone, but far and wide,
Across the Thames's gleaming tide,
To distant fields the blaze was borne ;
And daisy white and hoary thorn,
In borrowed lustre seemed to sham
The rose or red Sweet Wil-li-am.
　　To those who on the hills around
　　Beheld the flames from Drury's mound,
As from a lofty altar rise ;
　　It seemed that nations did conspire,
　　To offer to the god of fire
Some vast stupendous sacrifice !
The summoned firemen woke at call,
And hied them to their stations all.
Starting from short and broken snooze,
Each sought his ponderous hobnailed shoes ;

But first his worsted hosen plied,
Plush breeches next in crimson dyed,
  His nether bulk embraced ;
Then jacket thick of red or blue,
Whose massy shoulders gave to view
The badge of each respective crew,
  In tin or copper traced.
The engines thundered through the street,
Fire-hook, pipe, bucket, all complete,
And torches glared and clattering feet
  Along the pavement paced.

.   .   .   .   .   .

E'en Higginbottom now was posed,
For sadder scene was ne'er disclosed ;
Without, within, in hideous show,
  Devouring flames resistless glow,
And blazing rafters downward go,
And never halloo ' Heads below ! '
  Nor notice give at all :
The firemen, terrified, are slow
To bid the pumping torrent flow,
  For fear the roof should fall.
Back, Robins, back ! Crump, stand aloof!
  Whitford, keep near the walls !
Huggins, regard your own behoof,
For, lo ! the blazing rocking roof
  Down, down in thunder falls !
An awful pause succeeds the stroke,
And o'er the ruins volumed smoke,

Rolling around its pitchy shroud,
Concealed them from the astonished crowd.
At length the mist awhile was cleared,
When lo ! amid the wreck upreared
Gradual a moving head appeared,
   And Eagle firemen knew
'Twas Joseph Muggins, name revered,
   The foreman of their crew.
Loud shouted all in signs of woe,
'A Muggins to the rescue, ho !'
   And poured the hissing tide :
Meanwhile the Muggins fought amain,
And strove and struggled all in vain,
For, rallying but to fall again,
   He tottered, sunk, and died !
Did none attempt, before he fell,
To succour one they loved so well ?
Yes, Higginbottom did aspire
(His fireman's soul was all on fire)
   His brother chief to save ;
But ah ! his reckless generous ire
   Served but to share his grave !
'Mid blazing beams and scalding streams,
Through fire and smoke he dauntless broke,
   Where Muggins broke before.
But sulphury stench and boiling drench
Destroying sight, o'erwhelmed him quite ;
   He sunk to rise no more.
Still o'er his head, while Fate he braved,
His whizzing water-pipe he waved ;

'Whitford and Mitford, ply your pumps ;
You, Clutterbuck, come, stir your stumps ;
Why are you in such doleful dumps ?
A fireman, and afraid of bumps !
What are they feared on ? fools,—'od rot 'em !' '
Were the last words of Higginbottom !" . . . .

Canning and Frere, the two chief writers in
the "Anti-Jacobin," had great merit as writers of
parody. There is hardly a better one to be found
than the following on Southey's verses regarding
Henry Martin the Regicide, the fun of which is
readily apparent even to those who do not know
the original :

INSCRIPTION

(For the door of the cell in Newgate where Mrs. Brownrigg, the
Prentice-cide, was confined previous to her execution).

" For one long term, or e'er her trial came,
Here Brownrigg lingered.   Often have these cells
Echoed her blasphemies, as with shrill voice
She screamed for fresh Geneva.   Not to her
Did the blithe fields of Tothill, or thy street,
St. Giles, its fair varieties expand,
Till at the last, in slow-drawn cart, she went
To execution.   Dost thou ask her crime ?
She whipped two female prentices to death,
And hid them in the coal-hole.   For her mind
Shaped strictest plans of discipline.   Sage schemes !
Such as Lycurgus taught, when at the shrine

Of the Orthyan goddess he bade flog
The little Spartans ; such as erst chastised
Our Milton, when at college. For this act
Did Brownrigg swing. Harsh laws ! But time shall
  come
When France shall reign, and laws be all repealed."

The following felicitous parody on Wolfe's "Lines on the Burial of Sir John Moore" is taken from Thomas Hood :

" Not a laugh was heard, nor a joyous note,
  As our friend to the bridal we hurried ;
Not a wit discharged his farewell joke,
  As the bachelor went to be married.

We married him quickly to save his fright,
  Our heads from the sad sight turning ;
And we sighed as we stood by the lamp's dim light,
  To think him not more discerning.

To think that a bachelor free and bright,
  And shy of the sex as we found him,
Should there at the altar, at dead of night,
  Be caught in the snares that bound him.

Few and short were the words we said,
  Though of cake and wine partaking ;
We escorted him home from the scene of dread,
  While his knees were awfully shaking.

Slowly and sadly we marched adown
    From the top to the lowermost story;
And we have never heard from nor seen the poor man
    Whom we left alone in his glory."

Mr. Barham has also left us a parody on the same lines:

" Not a sou had he got,—not a guinea, or note,
    And he looked most confoundedly flurried,
As he bolted away without paying his shot,
    And the landlady after him hurried.

We saw him again at dead of night,
    When home from the club returning;
We twigged the Doctor beneath the light
    Of the gas lamp brilliantly burning.

All bare, and exposed to the midnight dews,
    Reclined in the gutter we found him,
And he looked like a gentleman taking a snooze,
    With his Marshall cloak around him.

' The Doctor is as drunk as the d—l,' we said,
    And we managed a shutter to borrow,
We raised him, and sighed at the thought that his head
    Would confoundedly ache on the morrow.

We bore him home and we put him to bed,
    And we told his wife and daughter

To give him next morning a couple of red
   Herrings with soda-water.

Loudly they talked of his money that's gone,
   And his lady began to upbraid him ;
But little he reck'd, so they let him snore on
   'Neath the counterpane, just as we laid him.

We tuck'd him in, and had hardly done,
   When beneath the window calling
We heard the rough voice of a son of a gun
   Of a watchman 'one o'clock' bawling.

Slowly and sadly we all walk'd down
   From his room on the uppermost story,
A rushlight we placed on the cold hearth-stone,
   And we left him alone in his glory."

In the examples which follow, the selection has
been made on the principle of giving only those of
which the prototypes are well known and will be
easily recognised, and here is another of Hood's,
written on a popular ballad :

"We met—'twas in a mob—and I thought he had done me—
  I felt—I could not feel—for no watch was upon me ;
  He ran—the night was cold—and his pace was unaltered,
  I too longed much to pelt—but my small-boned legs faltered.
  I wore my brand new boots—and unrivalled their brightness,
  They fit me to a hair—how I hated their tightness !
  I called, but no one came, and my stride had a tether,
  Oh, *thou* hast been the cause of this anguish, my leather !

And once again we met—and an old pal was near him,
He swore, a something low—but 'twas no use to fear him,
I seized upon his arm, he was mine and mine only,
And stept, as he deserved—to cells wretched and lonely :
And there he will be tried—but I shall ne'er receive her,
The watch that went too sure for an artful deceiver ;
The world may think me gay—heart and feet ache together,
Oh, *thou* hast been the cause of this anguish, my leather !"

Here is another upon an old favourite song :

THE BANDIT'S FATE.

" He wore a brace of pistols the night when first we met,
His deep-lined brow was frowning beneath his wig of jet,
His footsteps had the moodiness, his voice the hollow tone,
Of a bandit chief, who feels remorse, and tears his hair alone—
    I saw him but at half-price, but methinks I see him now,
    In the tableau of the last act, with the blood upon his brow.

A private bandit's belt and boots, when next we met, he wore ;
His salary, he told me, was lower than before ;
And standing at the O. P. wing he strove, and not in vain,
To borrow half a sovereign, which he never paid again.
    I saw it but a moment—and I wish I saw it now—
    As he buttoned up his pocket, with a condescending bow.

And once again we met ; but no bandit chief was there ;
His rouge was off, and gone that head of once luxuriant hair :
He lodges in a two-pair back, and at the public near,
He cannot liquidate his ' chalk,' or wipe away his beer.
    I saw him sad and seedy, yet methinks I see him now,
    In the tableau of the last act, with the blood upon his brow."

Goldsmith's " When lovely woman stoops to folly," has been thus parodied by Shirley Brooks :

" When lovely woman, lump of folly,
    Would show the world her vainest trait,—

Would treat herself as child her dolly,
And warn each man of sense away,—
The surest method she'll discover
To prompt a wink in every eye,
Degrade a spouse, disgust a lover,
And spoil a scalp-skin, is—to dye !"

Examples like these are numerous, and may be found in the "Bon Gaultier Ballads" of Theodore Martin and Professor Aytoun; "The Ingoldsby Legends" of Barham; and the works of Lewis Carroll.

One of the "Bon Gaultier" travesties was on Macaulay, and was called "The Laureate's Journey;" of which these two verses are part:

" 'He's dead, he's dead, the Laureate's dead !' Thus, thus the cry began,
And straightway every garret roof gave up its minstrel man ;
From Grub Street, and from Houndsditch, and from Farringdon Within,
The poets all towards Whitehall poured in with eldritch din.

Loud yelled they for Sir James the Graham : but sore afraid was he ;
A hardy knight were he that might face such a minstrelsie.
'Now by St. Giles of Netherby, my patron saint, I swear,
I'd rather by a thousand crowns Lord Palmerston were here !' "

It is necessary, however, to confine our quotations within reasonable limits, and a few from the modern writers must suffice. The next is by Henry S. Leigh, one of the best living writers of burlesque verse.

ONLY SEVEN.*

(A PASTORAL STORY, AFTER WORDSWORTH.)

"I marvelled why a simple child,
    That lightly draws its breath,
Should utter groans so very wild,
    And look as pale as death.

Adopting a parental tone,
    I asked her why she cried;
The damsel answered with a groan,
    'I've got a pain inside.

I thought it would have sent me mad,
    Last night about eleven.'
Said I, 'What is it makes you bad?
How many apples have you had?'
    She answered, 'Only seven!'

'And are you sure you took no more,
    My little maid,' quoth I.
'Oh, please, sir, mother gave me four,
    But they were in a pie.'

'If that's the case,' I stammered out,
    'Of course you've had eleven.'
The maiden answered with a pout,
    'I ain't had more nor seven!'

I wondered hugely what she meant,
    And said, 'I'm bad at riddles,

* From the "Carols of Cockayne."

But I know where little girls are sent
   For telling tarradiddles.

Now if you don't reform,' said I,
   You'll never go to heaven!'
But all in vain; each time I try,
The little idiot makes reply,
   'I ain't had more nor seven!'

POSTSCRIPT.

To borrow Wordsworth's name was wrong,
   Or slightly misapplied;
And so I'd better call my song,
   'Lines from Ache-inside.'"

Mr. Swinburne's alliterative style lays him particularly open to the skilful parodist, and he has been well imitated by Mr. Mortimer Collins, who, perhaps, is as well known as novelist as poet. The following example is entitled

"IF."

"If life were never bitter,
   And love were always sweet,
Then who would care to borrow
A moral from to-morrow?
If Thames would always glitter,
   And joy would ne'er retreat,
If life were never bitter,
   And love were always sweet.

If care were not the waiter,
  Behind a fellow's chair,
When easy-going sinners
Sit down to Richmond dinners,
And life's swift stream goes straighter—
  By Jove, it would be rare,
If care were not the waiter
  Behind a fellow's chair.

If wit were always radiant,
  And wine were always iced,
And bores were kicked out straightway
Through a convenient gateway :
Then down the year's long gradient
  'Twere sad to be enticed,
If wit were always radiant,
  And wine were always iced."

The next instance, by the same author, is another good imitation of Mr. Swinburne's style. It is a recipe for

SALAD.

"Oh, cool in the summer is salad,
  And warm in the winter is love ;
And a poet shall sing you a ballad
  Delicious thereon and thereof.
A singer am I, if no sinner,
  My muse has a marvellous wing,
And I willingly worship at dinner
  The sirens of spring.

Take endive—like love it is bitter,
　　Take beet—for like love it is red ;
Crisp leaf of the lettuce shall glitter
　　And cress from the rivulet's bed ;
Anchovies, foam-born, like the lady
　　Whose beauty has maddened this bard ;
And olives, from groves that are shady,
　　And eggs—boil 'em hard."

The "Shootover Papers," by members of the Oxford University, contains this parody, written upon the "Procuratores," a kind of university police :

"Oh, vestment of velvet and virtue,
　　Oh, venomous victors of vice,
Who hurt men who never hurt you,
　　Oh, calm, cold, crueller than ice.
Why wilfully wage you this war, is
　　All pity purged out of your breast ?
Oh, purse-prigging procuratores,
　　　　Oh, pitiless pest !

We had smote and made redder than roses,
　　With juice not of fruit nor of bud,
The truculent townspeople's noses,
　　And bathed brutal butchers in blood ;
And we all aglow in our glories,
　　Heard you not in the deafening din ;
And ye came, oh ye procuratores,
　　　　And ran us all in !"

In the same book a certain school of poets has been hit at in the following lines :

> " Mingled, aye, with fragrant yearnings,
>   Throbbing in the mellow glow,
> Glint the silvery spirit burnings,
>   Pearly blandishments of woe.
>
> Ay ! for ever and for ever,
>   While the love-lorn censers sweep ;
> While the jasper winds dissever,
>   Amber-like, the crystal deep ;
>
> Shall the soul's delicious slumber,
>   Sea-green vengeance of a kiss,
> Reach despairing crags to number
>   Blue infinities of bliss."

The " Diversions of the Echo Club," by Bayard Taylor, contains many parodies, principally upon American poets, and gives this admirable rendering of Edgar A. Poe's style :

THE PROMISSORY NOTE.

> " In the lonesome latter years,
>   (Fatal years !)
>   To the dropping of my tears
>   Danced the mad and mystic spheres
>   In a rounded, reeling rune,
>   'Neath the moon,
> To the dripping and the dropping of my tears.

Ah, my soul is swathed in gloom,
(Ulalume!)
In a dim Titanic tomb,
For my gaunt and gloomy soul
Ponders o'er the penal scroll,
O'er the parchment (not a rhyme),
Out of place,—out of time,—
I am shredded, shorn, unshifty,
(Oh, the fifty!)
And the days have passed, the three,
Over me!
And the debit and the credit are as one to him and me!

'Twas the random runes I wrote
At the bottom of the note
(Wrote and freely
Gave to Greeley),
In the middle of the night,
In the mellow, moonless night,
When the stars were out of sight,
When my pulses like a knell,
(Israfel!)
Danced with dim and dying fays
O'er the ruins of my days,
O'er the dimeless, timeless days,
When the fifty, drawn at thirty,
Seeming thrifty, yet the dirty
Lucre of the market, was the most that I could raise!

Fiends controlled it,
(Let him hold it!)

Devils held for me the inkstand and the pen ;
    Now the days of grace are o'er,
        (Ah, Lenore !)
I am but as other men :
What is time, time, time,
To my rare and runic rhyme,
To my random, reeling rhyme,
By the sands along the shore,
Where the tempest whispers, 'Pay him !' and I answer,
   'Nevermore !'" *

Bret Harte also has given a good imitation of Poe's style in " The Willows," from which there follows an extract :

  " But Mary, uplifting her finger,
    Said, 'Sadly this bar I mistrust,—
    I fear that this bar does not trust.
  Oh, hasten—oh, let us not linger—
    Oh, fly—let us fly—ere we must !'
  In terror she cried, letting sink her
    Parasol till it trailed in the dust,—
  In agony sobbed, letting sink her
    Parasol till it trailed in the dust,—
    Till it sorrowfully trailed in the dust.

  Then I pacified Mary and kissed her,
    And tempted her into the room,
    And conquered her scruples and gloom ;

* "'What do you mean by the reference to Greeley?'
"'I thought everybody had heard that Greeley's only autograph of Poe was a signature to a promissory note for fifty dollars. He offers to sell it for half the money.'"—*Diversions of the Echo Club.*

And we passed to the end of the vista,
　But were stopped by the warning of doom,—
By some words that were warning of doom.
　And I said, 'What is written, sweet sister,
　At the opposite end of the room?'
She sobbed as she answered, 'All liquors
　Must be paid for ere leaving the room.'"

Mr. Calverley is perhaps one of the best of the later parodists, and he hits off Tennyson, Mrs. Browning, Coventry Patmore, and others most inimitably. We give a couple of verses from one, a parody of his upon a well-known lyric of Tennyson's, and few we think after perusing it would be able to read "The Brook" without its murmur being associated with the wandering tinker:

　" I loiter down by thorp and town;
　　For any job I'm willing;
　　Take here and there a dusty brown
　　And here and there a shilling.

　.　　.　　.　　.　　.　　.　　.

Thus on he prattled, like a babbling brook,
Then I; 'The sun has slept behind the hill,
And my Aunt Vivian dines at half-past six.'
So in all love we parted: I to the Hall,
They to the village. It was noised next noon
That chickens had been missed at Syllabub Farm."

Mr. Tennyson's "Home they brought her warrior

dead," has likewise been differently travestied by various writers. One of these by Mr. Sawyer is given here :

The Recognition.

" Home they brought her sailor son,
 Grown a man across the sea,
Tall and broad and black of beard,
 And hoarse of voice as man may be.

Hand to shake and mouth to kiss,
 Both he offered ere he spoke ;
But she said, ' What man is this
 Comes to play a sorry joke ? '

Then they praised him—call'd him ' smart,'
 ' Tightest lad that ever stept ; '
But her son she did not know,
 And she neither smiled nor wept.

Rose, a nurse of ninety years,
 Set a pigeon-pie in sight ;
She saw him eat—''Tis he ! 'tis he !'—
 She knew him—by his appetite ! "

"The May-Queen" has also suffered in some verses called "The Biter Bit," of which these are the last four lines :

" You may lay me in my bed, mother—my head is throbbing sore ;
 And, mother, prithee let the sheets be duly aired before ;
 And if you'd do a kindness to your poor desponding child,
 Draw me a pot of beer, mother—and, mother, draw it mild ! "

Mr. Calverley has imitated well also the old ballad style, as in this one, of which we give the opening verses:

> " It was a railway passenger,
>   And he leapt out jauntilie.
>   ' Now up and bear, thou proud portèr,
>   My two chattels to me.
>
>   .   .   .   .   .
>
>   ' And fetch me eke a cabman bold,
>   That I may be his fare, his fare:
>   And he shall have a good shilling,
>   If by two of the clock he do me bring
>   To the terminus, Euston Square.'
>
>   ' Now,—so to thee the Saints alway,
>   Good gentlemen, give luck,—
>   As never a cab may I·find this day,
>   For the cabmen wights have struck:
>
>   And now, I wis, at the Red Post Inn,
>   Or else at the Dog and Duck,
>   Or at Unicorn Blue, or at Green Griffin,
>   The nut-brown ale and the fine old gin
>   Right pleasantlie they do suck.'" . . . .

The following imitation of the old ballad form is by Mr. Lewis Carroll, who has written many capital versions of different poems:

Ye Carpette Knyghte.

"I have a horse—a ryghte good horse—
    Ne doe I envie those
Who scoure ye plaine in headie course,
    Tyll soddaine on theyre nose
They lyghte wyth unexpected force—
    It ys—a horse of clothes.

I have a saddel—'Say'st thou soe?
    Wyth styrruppes, knyghte, to boote?'
I sayde not that—I answere 'Noe'—
    Yt lacketh such, I woot—
Yt ys a mutton-saddel, loe!
    Parte of ye fleecie brute.

I have a bytte—a right good bytte—
    As schall be seen in time.
Ye jawe of horse yt wyll not fytte—
    Yts use ys more sublyme.
Fayre Syr, how deemest thou of yt?
    Yt ys—thys bytte of rhyme."

In "Alice in Wonderland,"* by the same
gentleman, there is this new version of an old
nursery ditty:

"'Will you walk a little faster?' said a whiting to a snail,
    'There's a porpoise close behind us, and he's treading on
        my tail.
    See how eagerly the lobsters and the turtles all advance!
    They are waiting on the shingle—will you come and join
        the dance?

* Macmillan & Co., London.

Will you, won't you, will you, won't you, will you join the
    dance ?
Will you, won't you, will you, won't you, won't you join the
    dance?

'You can really have no notion how delightful it will be
When they take us up and throw us with the lobsters out
    to sea !'
But the snail replied, ' Too far, too far !' and gave a look
    askance,
Said he thanked the whiting kindly, but he would not join
    the dance.
Would not, could not, would not, could not, would not
    join the dance,
Would not, could not, would not, could not, could not join
    the dance.

'What matters it how far we go ?' his scaly friend replied ;
'There is another shore, you know, upon the other side.
The farther off from England the nearer is to France—
Then turn not pale, beloved snail, but come and join the
    dance ?
Will you, won't you, will you, won't you, will you join the
    dance ?
Will you, won't you, will you, won't you, won't you join
    the dance ?' "

Mr. Carroll's adaptation of " You are old, Father
William," is one of the best of its class, and here
are two verses :

" ' You are old, Father William,' the young man said,
    ' And your hair has become very white ;
And yet you incessantly stand on your head—
    Do you think, at your age, it is right ?'

'In my youth,' Father William replied to his son,
  'I feared it might injure the brain ;
But now I am perfectly sure I have none—
  Why, I do it again and again !'

'You are old,' said the youth, 'and your jaws are too
    weak
  For anything tougher than suet ;
Yet you finished the goose, with the bones and the
    beak—
  Pray, how do you manage to do it?'
'In my youth,' said his father, 'I took to the law,
  And argued each case with my wife ;
And the muscular strength which it gave to my jaw
  Has lasted the rest of my life.' " *

Mr. H. Cholmondeley-Pennell in "Puck on
Pegasus" gives some good examples, such as that
on the "Hiawatha" of Longfellow, the "Song of
In-the-Water," and also that on Southey's "How
the Waters come down at Lodore," the parody
being called "How the Daughters come down at
Dunoon," of which these are the concluding lines :

"Feathers a-flying all—bonnets untying all—
  Crinolines rapping and flapping and slapping all,
  Balmorals dancing and glancing entrancing all,—
        Feats of activity—
        Nymphs on declivity—

* See "Alice in Wonderland."

Sweethearts in ecstasies—
Mothers in vextasies—
Lady-loves whisking and frisking and clinging on,
True lovers puffing and blowing and springing on,
Flushing and blushing and wriggling and giggling on,
Teasing and pleasing and wheezing and squeezing on,
Everlastingly falling and bawling and sprawling on,
Flurrying and worrying and hurrying and skurrying on,
Tottering and staggering and lumbering and slithering
    on,
        Any fine afternoon
        About July or June—
      That's just how the Daughters
      Come down at Dunoon !"

"Twas ever thus," the well-known lines of Moore,
has also been travestied by Mr. H. C. Pennell:

"Wus ! ever wus ! By freak of Puck's
   My most exciting hopes are dashed;
I never wore my spotless ducks
   But madly—wildly—they were splashed !
I never roved by Cynthia's beam,
   To gaze upon the starry sky;
But some old stiff-backed beetle came,
   And charged into my pensive eye :

And oh ! I never did the swell
   In Regent Street, amongst the beaus,
But smuts the most prodigious fell,
   And always settled on my nose !"

Moore's lines have evidently been tempting to the parodists, for Mr. Calverley and Mr. H. S. Leigh have also written versions : Mr. Leigh's begins thus—

> " I never reared a young gazelle
>   (Because, you see, I never tried),
>   But had it known and loved me well,
>   No doubt the creature would have died.
>   My sick and aged Uncle John
>   Has known me long and loves me well,
>   But still persists in living on—
>   I would he were a young gazelle."

Shakespeare's soliloquy in Hamlet has been frequently selected as a subject for parody; the first we give being the work of Mr. F. C. Burnand in " Happy Thoughts " :

> " To sniggle or to dibble, that's the question !
>   Whether to bait a hook with worm or bumble,
>   Or to take up arms of any sea, some trouble
>   To fish, and then home send 'em. To fly—to whip—
>   To moor and tie my boat up by the end
>   To any wooden post, or natural rock
>   We may be near to, on a Preservation
>   Devoutly to be fished. To fly—to whip—
>   To whip ! perchance two bream ;—and there's the
>   chub !"

CREMATION.

"To Urn, or not to Urn? That is the question:
Whether 'tis better in our frames to suffer
The shows and follies of outrageous custom,
Or to take fire against a sea of zealots,
And, by consuming, end them? To Urn—to keep—
No more: and while we keep, to say we end
Contagion, and the thousand graveyard ills
That flesh is heir to—'tis a consume-ation
Devoutly to be wished! To burn—to keep—
To keep! Perchance to lose—ay, there's the rub!
For in the course of things what duns may come,
Or who may shuffle off our Dresden urn,
Must give us pause. There's the respect
That makes inter-i-ment of so long use;
For who would have the pall and plumes of hire,
The tradesman's prize—a proud man's obsequies,
The chaffering for graves, the legal fee,
The cemetery beadle, and the rest,
When he himself might his few ashes make
With a mere furnace? Who would tombstones bear,
And lie beneath a lying epitaph,
But that the dread of simmering after death—
That uncongenial furnace from whose burn
No incremate returns—weakens the will,
And makes us rather bear the graves we have
Than fly to ovens that we know not of?"

The next, on the same subject, is from an American source, where it is introduced by the remark:

"I suppose they'll be wanting us to change our language as well as our habits. Our years will have to be dated A.C., in the year of cremation; and 'from creation to cremation' will serve instead of 'from the cradle to the grave.' We may expect also some lovely elegies in the future—something in the following style perhaps, for, of course, when gravediggers are succeeded by pyre-lighters, the grave laments of yore will be replaced by lighter melodies "

"Above your mantel, in the new screen's shade,
    Where smokes the coal in one dull, smouldering
        heap,
  Each in his patent urn for ever laid,
    The baked residue of our fathers sleep.

The wheezy call of muffins in the morn,
    The milkman tottering from his rushy sled,
The help's shrill clarion, or the fishman's horn,
    No more shall rouse them from their lofty bed.

For them no more the blazing fire-grate burns,
    Or busy housewife fries her savoury soles,
Though children run to clasp their sires' red urns,
    And roll them in a family game of bowls.

Perhaps in this deserted pot is laid
    Some heart once pregnant with celestial fire,
Hands that the rod paternal may have swayed,
    Or waked to ecstasy the living liar."

The well-known lady traveller, Mrs. Burton, in one of her volumes gives the following amusing verses :

"What is the black man saying,
   Brother, the whole day long?
Methinks I hear him praying
   Ever the self-same song—
   Sa'b meri bakshish do!

Brother, they are not praying,
   They are not doing so ;
The only thing they're saying
   Is *sa'b meri bakshish do.*
   (Gi'e me a 'alfpenny do.)

To give specimens of all the kinds of parody were impossible, and we can only refer to the prose parodies of Thackeray's " Novels by Eminent Hands," and Bret Harte's "Condensed Novels." *
Renderings of popular ballads in this way are common enough in our comic periodicals, as *Punch, Fun,* &c. Indeed, one appeared in *Punch* a number of years ago, called "Ozokerit," a travesty of Tennyson's " In Memoriam," which has been considered one of the finest ever written. They are to be found, too, in many of those Burlesques and Extra-

---

* Reference may also be made here to a recent work, "The Heptalogia ; or the Seven against Sense," a book wholly devoted to parody, the merits of which could not be shown by extracts, but requires to be read at length to be properly estimated.

vaganzas which are put upon the stage now, and
these the late Mr. Planchè had a delightful faculty
of writing, the happiness and ring of which have
rarely been equalled. Take, for instance, one
verse of a parody in "Jason" on a well-known air
in the "Waterman:"

> "Now farewell my trim-built Argo,
>   Greece and Fleece and all, farewell,
>   Never more as supercargo
>   Shall poor Jason cut a swell."

And here is the opening verse of another song
by the same author:

> "When other lips and other eyes
>   Their tales of love shall tell,
>   Which means the usual sort of lies
>   You've heard from many a swell;
>   When, bored with what you feel is bosh,
>   You'd give the world to see
>   A friend whose love you know will wash,
>   Oh, then, remember me!"

Another very popular song has been parodied
in this way by Mr. Carroll:

> "Beautiful soup, so rich and green,
>   Waiting in a big tureen!
>   Who for such dainties would not stoop!
>   Soup of the evening, beautiful soup!
>   Soup of the evening, beautiful soup!"

American papers put in circulation many little verses, such as this—

> "The melancholy days have come,
>   The saddest of the year ;
> Too warm, alas ! for whiskey punch,
>   Too cold for lager beer."

And this, in reference to the Centennial Exhibition :

> "Breathes there a Yank, so mean, so small,
> Who never says, 'Wall, now, by Gaul,
> I reckon since old Adam's fall
> There's never growed on this 'ere ball
> A nation so all-fired tall
>   As we centennial Yankees."

A number of periodicals nowadays make parody and other out-of-the-way styles of literary composition a feature in their issues by way of competition for prizes, and one of these is given here. The author signs himself " Hermon," and the poem was selected by the editor of " Truth " (November 25, 1880) for a prize in a competition of parodies upon " Excelsior." It is called "That Thirty-four ! " having reference, it is perhaps hardly necessary to state, to the American puzzle of that name which has proved so perplexing an affair to some people.

That Thirty-four.

"Chill August's storms were piping loud,
When through a gaping London crowd,
There passed a youth, who still was heard
To mutter the perplexing word,
               ' That Thirty-four !'

His eyes were wild ; his brow above
Was crumpled like an old kid-glove ;
And like some hoarse crow's grating note
That word still quivered in his throat,
               ' That Thirty-four !'

' Oh, give it up !' his comrades said ;
' It only muddles your poor head ;
It is not worth your finding out.'
He answered with a wailing shout,
               ' That Thirty-four !'

' Art not content,' the maiden said,
' To solve the " Fifteen "-one instead ?'
He paused—his tearful eyes he dried—
Gulped down a sob, then sadly sighed,
               ' That Thirty-four !'

At midnight, on their high resort,
The cats were startled at their sport
To hear, beneath one roof, a tone
Gasp out, betwixt a snore and groan,
               ' That Thirty-four !'"

HIS ingenious style of versification, where the last word or phrase in each line is taken for the beginning of the next, is sometimes also called "Concatenation" verse. The invention of this mode of composition is claimed by M. Lasphrise, a French poet, who wrote the following:

> " Falloit-il que le ciel me rendit amoreux,
> Amoreux, jouissant d'une beauté craintive,
> Craintive à recevoir la douceur excessive,
> Excessive au plaisir que rend l'amant heureux?
> Heureux si nous avions quelques paisibles lieux,
> Lieux où plus surement l'ami fidèle arrive,
> Arrive sans soupçon de quelque ami attentive,
> Attentive à vouloir nous surprendre tous deux."

The poem which follows is from a manuscript furnished by an American gentleman, who states that he has never seen it in print, and knows not

the author's name. The "rhythm somewhat re-
sembles the ticking of a clock," from whence the
poem derives its name of

THE MUSICAL CLOCK.

" Wing the course of time with music,
   Music of the grand old days—
   Days when hearts were brave and noble,
   Noble in their simple ways.
   Ways, however rough, yet earnest,
   Earnest to promote the truth—
   Truth that teaches us a lesson,
   Lesson worthy age and youth.
   Youth and age alike may listen—
   Listen, meditate, improve—
   Improve in happiness and glory,
   Glory that shall Heavenward move.
   Move, as music moves, in pathos,
   Pathos sweet, and power sublime,
   Sublime to raise the spirit drooping,
   Drooping with the toils of time.
   Time reveals, amid its grandeur,
   Grandeur purer, prouder still—
   Still revealing dreams of beauty,
   Beauty that inspires the will—
   Will a constant sighing sorrow,
   Sorrow full of tears restore,
   Restore but for a moment, pleasure ?
   Pleasure dead can live no more.

No more, then, languish for the buried,
Buried calmly let it be.
Be the star of promise Heaven,
Heaven has sweeter joys for thee.
For thee perchance, though dark the seeming,
Seeming dark, may yet prove bright,
Bright through mortal cares, shall softly,
Softly dissipate the night.
Night shall not endure for ever,—
Ever! no, the laws of Earth,
Earth inconstant, shall forbid it—
Bid it change from gloom to mirth.
Mirth and grief, are light and shadow—
Shadows light to us are dear.
Dear the scene becomes by contrast—
Contrast there, in beauty here.
Here, through sun and tempest many,
Many shall thy being pass—
Pass without a sigh of sorrow,
Sorrow wins not by alas!
Alas! we pardon in a maiden,
Maiden when her heart is young,
Young and timid, but in manhood,
Manhood should be sterner strung,
Strung as though his nerves were iron,
Iron tempered well to bend—
Bend, mayhap, but yielding never,
Never, when despair would rend —
Rend the pillars from the temple,
Temple in the human breast,

Breast that lonely grief has chosen,
Chosen for her place of rest—
Rest unto thy spirit, only,
Only torment will she bring.
Bring, oh man ! the lyre of gladness,
Gladness frights the harpy's wing !"

The following two pieces are similar in style to some of our seventeenth-century poets :

AD MORTEM.

" The longer life, the more offence ;
　The more offence, the greater pain ;
　The greater pain, the less defence ;
　The less defence, the greater gain—
　　　　Wherefore, come death, and let me die !

　The shorter life, less care I find,
　Less care I take, the sooner over ;
　The sooner o'er, the merrier mind ;
　The merrier mind, the better lover—
　　　　Wherefore, come death, and let me die !

　Come, gentle death, the ebb of care ;
　The ebb of care, the flood of life ;
　The flood of life, I'm sooner there ;
　I'm sooner there—the end of strife—
　The end of strife, that thing wish I—
　　　　Wherefore, come death, and let me die !"

TRUTH.

"Nerve thy soul with doctrines noble,
　Noble in the walks of time,
Time that leads to an eternal
　An eternal life sublime ;
Life sublime in moral beauty,
　Beauty that shall ever be ;
Ever be to lure thee onward,
　Onward to the fountain free—
Free to every earnest seeker,
　Seeker for the Fount of Youth—
Youth exultant in its beauty,
　Beauty of the living truth."

The following hymn appears in the Irish Church
Hymnal, and is by Mr. J. Byrom :

"My spirit longs for Thee
　　Within my troubled breast,
　Though I unworthy be
　　Of so Divine a Guest.

　Of so Divine a Guest
　　Unworthy though I be,
　Yet has my heart no rest,
　　Unless it come from Thee.

　Unless it come from Thee,
　　In vain I look around ;

In all that I can see
No rest is to be found.

No rest is to be found.
But in Thy blessèd love ;
Oh, let my wish be crowned
And send it from above."

Dr., as he was commonly called, Byrom, seems
to have been an amiable and excellent man, and
his friends after his death in September 1763 col-
lected and published all the verses of his they
could lay hands on, in 2 vols. 12mo, at Manchester
in 1773. A more complete edition was issued in
1814. Many of Byrom's poems evince talent, but
a great part are only calculated for private perusal :
his "Diary" and "Remains" were published by
the Chetham Society (1854-57). Byrom was the
inventor of a successful system of shorthand. He
was a decided Jacobite, and his mode of defending
his sentiments on this point are still remembered
and quoted :

"God bless the King ! I mean the Faith's defender ;
God bless—no harm in blessing—the Pretender !
But who Pretender is, or who the King,
God bless us all—that's quite another thing !"

ACARONIC verse is properly a system of Latin inflections joined to words of a modern vernacular, such as English, French, German, &c.; some writers, however, choose to disregard the strictness of this definition, and consider everything macaronic which is written with the aid of more than one language or dialect. Dr. Geddes (born 1737; died 1802), considered one of the greatest of English macaronic writers, says: " It is the characteristic of a Macaronic poem to be written in Latin hexameters ; but so as to admit occasionally vernacular words, either in their native form, or with a Latin inflection—other licenses, too, are allowed in the measure of the lines, contrary to the strict rules of prosody." Broad enough reservations these, of which Dr. Geddes in his own works was not slow in availing himself, and as will be seen in the specimens given, his example has been well followed, for the strict rule that an English macaronic should consist of the vernacular made classical with Latin terminations has been as much honoured in the breach as in the observance. Another characteristic in macaronics is that these poems recognise no law in orthography, etymology, syntax, or prosody. The examples which here follow are confined exclusively to those which have their basis, so to speak, in the English language, and, with the exception of a few of the earlier ones, the majority of the selections in this volume have their origin in our own times.

" The earliest collection of English Christmas carols supposed to have been published," says Hone's " Every Day Book," " is only known from the last leaf of a volume printed by Wynkyn Worde in 1521. There are two carols upon it : ' A Carol of Huntynge ' is reprinted in the last edition of Juliana Berners' ' Boke of St. Alban's ; ' the other, ' A carol of bringing in the Bore's Head,' is in Dibdin's edition of ' Ames,' with a copy of the carol as it is now sung in Queen's College, Oxford, every Christmas Day." Dr. Bliss of Oxford printed a few copies of this for private circulation, together with Anthony Wood's version of it. The version subjoined is from a collection imprinted at London, " in the Poultry, by Richard Kele, dwelling at the long shop vnder Saynt Myldrede's Chyrche," about 1546:

A Carol bringing in the Bore's Head.

" Caput apri defero
Reddens laudes Domino.
The bore's heed in hande bring I,
With garlands gay and rosemary,
I pray you all synge merelye
Qui estis in convivio.

The bore's heed I understande
Is the thefte service in this lande,
Take wherever it be fande,
Servite cum cantico.
Be gladde lordes both more and lasse,
For this hath ordeyned our stewarde,
To cheere you all this Christmasse,
The bore's heed with mustarde.
Caput apri defero
Reddens laudes Domino.''

Another version of the last verse is:

" Our steward hath provided this
In honour of the King of Bliss:
Which on this day to be served is,
In Regimensi Atrio.
Caput apri defero
Reddens laudes Domino."

Skelton, who was the poet-laureate about the end of the fifteenth century, has in his " Boke of Colin Clout," and also in that of " Philip Sparrow," much macaronic verse, as in " Colin Clout," when he is speaking of the priests of those days, he says :

> " Of suche vagabundus
> Speaking totus mundus,
> How some syng let abundus,
> At euerye ale stake
> With welcome hake and make,
> By the bread that God brake,
> I am sory for your sake.
> I speake not of the god wife
> But of their apostles lyfe,
> Cum ipsis vel illis
> Qui manent in villis
> Est uxor vel ancilla,
> Welcome Jacke and Gilla,
> My prety Petronylla,
> An you wil be stilla
> You shall haue your willa,
> Of such pater noster pekes
> All the world speakes," &c.

In Harsnett's " Detection " are some curious lines, being a curse for " the miller's eeles that were stolne ":

" All you that stolne the miller's eeles,
   Laudate dominum de cœlis,
   And all they that have consented thereto,
   Benedicamus domino."

In "Literary Frivolities" there was a notice of
and quotation from Ruggles' *jeu d'esprit* of "Ignoramus," and here follows a short scene from this play,
containing a humorous burlesque of the old Nor-
man Law-Latin, in which the elder brethren of the
legal profession used to plead, and in which the
old Reporters come down to the Bar of to-day—if,
indeed, that venerable absurdity can be caricatured.
It would be rather difficult to burlesque a system
that provided for a writ *de pipâ vini carriandâ*—
that is, "for negligently carrying a pipe of wine !"

IGNORAMUS.

ACTUS I.—SCENA III.

ARGUMENTUM.

IGNORAMUS, clericis suis vocatis DULMAN & PECUS, amorem suum
   erga ROSABELLAM narrat, irredetque MUSÆUM quasi hominem
   academicum.

Intrant IGNORAMUS, DULMAN, PECUS, MUSÆUS.

Igno. Phi, phi : tanta pressa, tantum croudum, ut fui
pene trusus ad mortem. Habebo actionem de intrusione
contra omnes et singulos. Aha Mounsieurs, voulez voz

intruder par joint tenant? il est playne case, il est point droite de le bien seance. O valde caleor: O chaud, chaud, chaud : precor Deum non meltavi meum pingue. Phi, phi. In nomine Dei, ubi sunt clerici mei jam? Dulman, Dulman.

Dul. Hic, Magister Ignoramus, vous avez Dulman.

Igno. Meltor, Dulman, meltor. Rubba me cum towallio, rubba. Ubi est Pecus?

Pec. Hìc, Sir.

Igno. Fac ventum, Pecus. Ita, sic, sic. Ubi est Fledwit?

Dul. Non est inventus.

Igno. Ponite nunc chlamydes vestras super me, ne capiam frigus. Sic, sic. Ainsi, bien faict. Inter omnes pœnas meas, valde lætor, et gaudeo nunc, quod feci bonum aggreamentum, inter Anglos nostros : aggreamentum, quasi aggregatio mentium. Super inde cras hoysabimus vela, et retornabimus iterum erga Londinum : tempus est, nam huc venimus Octabis Hillarii, et nunc fere est Quindena Pasche.

Dul. Juro, magister, titillasti punctum legis hodie.

Igno. Ha, ha, he! Puto titillabam. Si le nom del granteur, ou granté soit rased, ou interlined en faict pol, le faict est grandement suspicious.

Dul. Et nient obstant, si faict pol, &c., &c. Oh illud etiam in Covin.

Igno. Ha, ha, he!

Pec. At id, de un faict pendu en le smoak, nunquam audivi titillatum melius.

Igno. Ha, ha, he! Quid tu dicis, Musæe?

Mus. Equidem ego parum intellexi.

Igno. Tu es gallicrista, vocatus a coxcomb; nunquam faciam te Legistam.

Dul. Nunquam, nunquam; nam ille fuit Universitans.

Igno. Sunt magni idiotæ, et clerici nihilorum, isti Universitantes: miror quomodo spendisti tuum tempus inter eos.

Mus. Ut plurimum versatus sum in Logicâ.

Igno. Logica? Quæ villa, quod burgum est Logica?

Mus. Est una artium liberalium.

Igno. Liberalium? Sic putabam. In nomine Dei, stude artes parcas et lucrosas : non est mundus pro artibus liberalibus jam.

Mus. Deditus etiam fui amori Philosophiæ.

Igno. Amori? Quid! Es pro bagaschiis et strumpetis? Si custodis malam regulam, non es pro me, sursum reddam te in manus parentum iterum.

Mus. Dii faxint.

Igno. Quota est clocka nunc?

Dul. Est inter octo et nina.

Igno. Inter octo et nina? Ite igitur ad mansorium nostrum cum baggis et rotulis.—Quid id est? videam hoc instrumentum; mane petit, dum calceo spectacula super nasum. O ho, ho, scio jam. Hæc indentura, facta, &c., inter Rogerum Rattledoke de Caxton in comitatu Brecknocke, &c. O ho, Richard Fen, John Den. O ho, Proud Buzzard, plaintiff, adversus Peake-

E

goose, defendant.　O ho, vide hic est defalta literæ;
emenda, emenda; nam in nostra lege una comma
evertit totum Placitum.　Ite jam, copiato tu hoc, tu hoc
ingrossa, tu Universitans trussato sumptoriam pro jorneâ.

[Exeunt Clerici.

IGNORAMUS solus.

Hi, ho!　Rosabella, hi ho!　Ego nunc eo ad Veneris
curiam letam, tentam hic apud Torcol: Vicecomes ejus
Cupido nunquam cessavit, donec invenit me in balivâ
suâ: Primum cum amabam Rosabellam nisi parvum,
misit parvum Cape, tum magnum Cape, et post, alias
Capias et pluries Capias, & Capias infinitas; & sic misit
tot Capias, ut tandem capavit me ut legatum ex omni sensu
et ratione meâ.　Ita sum sicut musca sine caput; buzzo &
turno circumcirca, et nescio quid facio.　Cum scribo
instrumentum, si femina nominatur, scribo Rosabellam;
pro Corpus cum causâ, corpus cum caudâ; pro Noverint
universi, Amaverint universi; pro habere ad rectum,
habere ad lectum; et sic vasto totum instrumentum.
Hei, ho! ho, hei, ho!

The following song by O'Keefe, is a mixture of
English, Latin, and nonsense:

" Amo, amas,

I love a lass,

As cedar tall and slender;

Sweet cowslip's grace

Is her nominative case,

And she's of the feminine gender.

Chorus.

Rorum, corum, sunt di-vorum,
    Harum, scarum, divo ;
Tag-rag, merry-derry, periwig and hatband,
    Hic, hoc, horum genitivo.

Can I decline a nymph so divine ?
    Her voice like a flute is dulcis ;
Her oculus bright, her manus white
    And soft, when I tacto her pulse is.
                    Chorus.

O how bella, my puella
    I'll kiss in secula seculorum ;
If I've luck, sir, she's my uxor,
    O dies benedictorum."
                    Chorus.

Of the many specimens written by the witty and versatile Dr. Maginn we select this on

THE SECOND EPODE OF HORACE.

" Blest man, who far from busy hum,
    Ut prisca gens mortalium,
Whistles his team afield with glee
    Solutus omni fenore ;
He lives in peace, from battles free,
    Neq' horret irratúm mare ;
And shuns the forum, and the gay
    Potentiorum limina,

Therefore to vines of purple gloss
Atlas maritat populos.
Or pruning off the boughs unfit
Feliciores inserit ;
Or, in a distant vale at ease
Prospectat errantes greges ;
Or honey into jars conveys
Aut tondet infirmas oves.
When his head decked with apples sweet
Auctumnus agris extulit,
At plucking pears he's quite *au fait*
Certant, et uvam purpuræ.
Some for Priapus, for thee some
Sylvare, tutor finium !
Beneath an oak 'tis sweet to be
Mod' in tenaci gramine :
The streamlet winds in flowing maze ;
Queruntur in silvis aves ;
The fount in dulcet murmur plays
Somnos quod invitet leves.
But when winter comes, (and that
Imbres nivesque comparat,)
With dogs he forces oft to pass
Apros in obstantes plagas ;
Or spreads his nets so thick and close
Turdis edacibus dolos ;
Or hares, or cranes, from far away
Jucunda captat præmia :
The wooer, love's unhappy stir,
Hæc inter obliviscitur,

His wife can manage without loss
Domum et parvos liberos ;
(Suppose her Sabine, or the dry
Pernicis uxor Appali,)
Who piles the sacred hearthstone high
Lassi sub adventúm viri,
And from his ewes, penned lest they stray,
Distenta siccet ubera ;
And this year's wine disposed to get
Dapes inemtas apparet.
Oysters to me no joys supply,
Magisve rhombus, aut scari,
(If when the east winds boisterous be
Hiems ad hoc vertat mare ;)
Your Turkey pout is not to us,
Non attagen Ionicus,
So sweet as what we pick at home
Oliva ramis arborum !
Or sorrel, which the meads supply,
Malvæ salubres corpori—
Or lamb, slain at a festal show
Vel hædus ereptus lupo.
Feasting, 'tis sweet the creature's dumb,
Videre prop'rantes domum,
Or oxen with the ploughshare go,
Collo trahentes languido ;
And all the slaves stretched out at ease,
Circum renidentes Lares !
Alphius the usurer, babbled thus,
Jam jam futurus rusticus,

Called in his cast on th' Ides—but he
Quærit Kalendis ponere !"

There is a little bit by Barham ("Ingoldsby
Legends") which is worthy of insertion:

" What Horace says is
Eheu fugaces
Anni labuntur, Postume! Postume!
Years glide away and are lost to me—lost to me !
Now when the folks in the dance sport their merry toes,
Taglionis and Ellslers, Duvernays and Ceritos,
Sighing, I murmured, 'O mihi pretæritos!'"

The following bright *carmen Macaronicum* appeared in an American periodical in 1873:

REX MIDAS.

" Vivit a rex in Persia land,
 A potens rex was he ;
Suum imperium did extend
 O'er terra and o'er sea.

Rex Midas habuit multum gold,
 Tamen he wanted plus ;
' Non satis est,' his constant cry—
 Ergo introit fuss.

Silenus was inebrius,—
 Id est, was slightly tight,
As he went vagus through the urbs,
 It was a tristis sight.

Rex Midas equitavit past
　On suum dromedary,
Vidit Silenus on his spree,
　Sic lætus et sic merry.

His costume was a wreath of leaves,
　And those were multum battered ;
Urchins had stoned him, and the ground
　Cum lachrymis was scattered.

Rex Midas picked hunc senem up,
　And put him on his pony,
Et bore him ad castellum grand
　Quod cost him multum money.

Dedit Silenum mollem care :
　Cum Bacchus found his ubi
Promisit Midas quod he asked.
　Rex Midas fuit—booby.

For aurum was his gaudium,
　Rogavit he the favour
Ut quid he touched might turn to gold ;
　Ab this he'd nunquam never.

Carpsit arose to try the charm,
　Et in eodem minute
It mutat into flavum gold,
　Ridet as spectat in it.

His filia rushed to meet her sire,
　He osculavit kindly ;

She lente stiffened into gold—
  Vidit he'd acted blindly.

Spectavit on her golden form,
  And in his brachia caught her:
'Heu me! sed tamen breakfast waits,
  My daughter, oh! my daughter!'

Venit ad suum dining-hall,
  Et coffeam gustavit,
Liquatum gold his fauces burned,—
  Loud he vociferavit:

'Triste erat amittere
  My solam filiam true,
Pejus to lose my pabulam.
  Eheu! Eheu!! Eheu!!!'

Big lachrymæ bedewed his cheeks—
  'O potens Bacchus lazy,
Prende ab me the power you gave,
  Futurum, ut I'll praise thee.'

Benignus Bacchus audiens groans,
  Misertus est our hero;
Dixit ut the Pactolian waves
  Ab hoc would cleanse him—vero.

Infelix rex was felix then,
  Et cum hilarious grin,
Ruit unto the river's bank,
  Et fortis plunged in.

The nefas power was washed away ;
   Sed even at this hour
Pactolus' sands are tinged with gold,
   Testes of Bacchus' power.

A tristis sed a sapiens vir
   Rex Midas fuit then ;
Et gratus to good Bacchus said,
   ' Non feram sic again.'

Hæc fable docet, plain to see,
   Quamquam the notion's old,
Hoc verum est, ut girls and grub
   Much melior sunt than gold."

The following well-known lines are from the "Comic Latin Grammar," a remarkably clever and curious work, full of quaint illustrations :

" Patres conscripti—took a boat and went to Philippi.
Trumpeter unus erat qui coatum scarlet habebat,
Stormum surgebat, et boatum overset—ebat,
Omnes drownerunt, quia swimaway non potuerunt,
Excipe John Periwig tied up to the tail of a dead pig."

A Treatise on Wine.

" The best tree, if ye take intent,
   Inter ligna fructifera,
Is the vine tree by good argument,
   Dulcia ferens pondera.

Saint Luke saith in his Gospel,
  Arbor fructu noscitur,
The vine beareth wine as I you tell,
  Hinc aliis præponitur.

The first that planted the vineyard
  Manet in cœlio gaudio,
His name was Noe, as I am learned
  Genesis testimonio.

God gave unto him knowledge and wit,
  A quo procedunt omnia,
First of the grape wine for to get
  Propter magna mysteria.

The first miracle that Jesus did,
  Erat in vino rubeo,
In Cana of Galilee it betide
  Testante Evangelio.

He changed water into wine
  Aquæ rubescunt hydriæ,
And bade give it to Archetcline,
  Ut gustet tunc primarie.

Like as the rose exceedeth all flowers,
  Inter cuncta florigera,
So doth wine all other liquors,
  Dans multa salutifera.

David, the prophet, saith that wine
  Lætificat cor hominis,

It maketh men merry if it be fine,
    Est ergo digni nominis.

It nourisheth age if it be good,
    Facit ut esset juvenis,
It gendereth in us gentle blood,
    Nam venas purgat sanguinis.

By all these causes, ye should think
    Quæ sunt rationabiles,
That good wine should be the best of drink,
    Inter potus potabiles.

Wine drinkers all, with great honour,
    Semper laudate Dominum,
The which sendeth the good liquor
    Propter salutem hominum.

Plenty to all that love good wine
    Donet Deus larguis,
And bring them some when they go hence,
    Ubi non sitient amplius."

                    —*Richard Hilles* (1535).

The two which follow are identical in theme, and show that the wags and wits of about thirty years ago were busy poking their fun at what was then their latest sensation, much as they do now. They both treat of the Sea-serpent; the first being from an American source :

THE SEA-SERPENT.

"Sed tempus necessit, and this was all over,
Cum illi successit another gay rover,
Nam cum navigaret, in his own cutter
Portentum apparet, which made them all flutter.

Est horridus anguis which they behold;
Haud dubio sanguis within them ran cold;
Trigenta pedes his head was upraised
Et corporis sedes in secret was placed.

Sic serpens manebat, so says the same joker,
Et sese ferebat as stiff as a poker;
Tergum fricabat against the old lighthouse;
Et sese liberabat of scaly detritus.

Tunc plumbo percussit, thinking he hath him,
At serpens exsiluit full thirty fathom;
Exsiluit mare with pain and affright,
Conatus abnare as fast as he might.

Neque illi secuti—no, nothing so rash,
Terrore sunt multi, he'd make such a splash,
Sed nunc adierunt, the place to inspect,
Et squamus viderunt, the which they collect.

Quicunque non credat aut doubtfully rails
Ad locum accedat, they'll show him the scales,
Quas, sola trophæa, they brought to the shore,—
Et causa est ea they couldn't get more."

The Death of the Sea-Serpent.

BY PUBLIUS JONATHAN VIRGILIUS JEFFERSON SMITH.

" Arma virumque cano, qui first in Monongahela
Tarnally squampushed the sarpent, mittens horrentia tella,
Musa, look sharp with your banjo ! I guess to relate this event, I
Shall need all the aid you can give ; so nunc aspirate canenti.
Mighty slick were the vessels progressing, jactata per æquora
    ventis,
But the brow of the skipper was sad, cum solicitudine mentis ;
For whales had been scarce in those parts, and the skipper, so long
    as he'd known her,
Ne'er had gathered less oil in a cruise to gladden the heart of her
    owner.
' Darn the whales,' cried the skipper at length, with a telescope
    forte videbo
Aut pisces, aut terras.   While speaking, just two or three points
    on the lee bow,
He saw coming toward them as fast as though to a combat 'twould
    tempt 'em,
A monstrum horrendum informe (qui lumen was shortly ademptum),
On the taffrail up jumps in a hurry, dux fortis, and seizing a trumpet,
Blows a blast that would waken the dead, mare turbat et æra
    rumpit—
' Tumble up, all you lubbers,' he cries, ' tumble up, for careering
    before us
Is the real old sea-sarpent himself, cristis maculisque decorus.'
' Consarn it,' cried one of the sailors, ' if e'er we provoke him he'll
    kill us,
He'll certainly chaw up hos morsu, et longis, implexibus illos.'
Loud laughs the bold skipper, and quick premit alto corde
    dolorem ;
(If he does feel like running, he knows it won't do to betray it
    before 'em.)
' O socii,' inquit.   ' I'm sartin you're not the fellers to funk, or
Shrink from the durem certamen, whose fathers fit bravely at
    Bunker ;

You, who have waged with the bears, and the buffalo, prœlia dura,
Down to the freshets and licks of our own free enlightened Missourer;
You, who could whip your own weight, catulis sævis sine telo,
Get your eyes skinned in a twinkling, et ponite tela phæsello!'
Talia voce refert, curisque ingentibus æger,
Marshals his cute little band, now panting their foe to beleaguer.
Swiftly they lower the boats, and swiftly each man at the oar is,
Excipe Britanni timidi duo, virque coloris.
(Blackskin, you know, never feels how sweet 'tis pro patri mori ;
Ovid had him in view when he said ' Nimium ne crede colori.')
Now swiftly they pull towards the monster, who seeing the cutter
    and gig nigh,
Glares at them with terrible eyes, suffectis sanguine et igni,
And, never conceiving their chief will so quickly deal him a floorer,
Opens wide to receive them at once, his linguis vibrantibis ora ;
But just as he's licking his lips, and gladly preparing to taste 'em,
Straight into his eyeball the skipper stridentem conjicit hastam.
Straight as he feels in his eyeball the lance, growing mightily sulky,
At 'em he comes in a rage, ora minax, lingua trusulca.
' Starn all,' cry the sailors at once, for they think he has certainly
    caught 'em,
Præsentemque viris intentant omnia mortem.
But the bold skipper exclaims, ' O terque quaterque beati !
Now with a will dare viam, when I want you, be only parati ;
This hoss feels like raising his hair, and in spite of his scaly old
    cortex,
Full soon you shall see that his corpse rapidus vorat æquore vortex.'
Hoc ait, and choosing a lance, ' With this one I think I shall
    hit it,'
He cries, and straight into his mouth, ad intima viscera millit,
Screeches the creature in pain, and writhes till the sea is com-
    motum,
As if all its waves had been lashed in a tempest per Eurum et Notum.
Interea terrible shindy Neptunus sensit, et alto
Prospiciens sadly around, wiped his eye with the cuff of his paletôt ;
And, mad at his favourite's fate, of oaths uttered one or two thousand,
Such as ' Corpo di Bacco ! Mehercle ! Sacre ! Mille Tonnerres !
    Potztausend !'

But the skipper, who thought it was time to this terrible fight dare
   finem,
With a scalping knife jumps on the neck of the snake secat et dextrâ
   crinem,
And, hurling the scalp in the air, half mad with delight to pos-
   sess it,
Shouts, ' Darn it—I've fixed up his flint, for in ventos vita recessit!'"
                                                    —*Punch.*

St. George et His Dragon.

" Hæc fabulam's one of those stories,
      Which the Italians say, 'ought to be true,'
   Sed which modern wiseacres have scattered
      Among les Illusions Perdus !

St. George eques errans erat
      Qui vibrat a seven-foot sword,
   Und er würde eher be all up a tree,
      Than be caught a-breaking his word.

Assuetus au matin to ride out
      Pour chercher quelquechose for to lick,
   Cap à pie en harness—and to see him
      Whack a rusticus pauvre was chic.

Perequitat thousands of peasants,
      Et mantled in armour complete—
   Cædat the whole huddle confestim
      Et could make them ausgespielt.

Si ce n'est que, sans doute, they were willing,
      To get up and solemnly swear
   That the very last Fraulein he'd seen was
      La plus belle dans tout la terre.

Ein Morgen he saw à le trottoir
  Puella formosissima très
Implicans amplexus Draconæ,
  So she couldn't get out of his way.

The dragon—donc voilà le tableau !
  Had eyes sanguine suffectis
Alæ comme les lutins in 'Paradise Lost,'
  Et was, on the whole, insuavis.

For Beauté miserable was there ever
  Eques who would not do and die ?
St. George his *h*astam projecit
  Right into the dragon—his eye !

Il coupe sa tête mit sein Schwert gut—
  Ses ailes, il coupe mit sein coûteau
Il coupe sa queu mit his hache des arms,
  Et la demoiselle let go.

In genua procumbit the ladye,
  Et dixit, ' You've saved my life—
Pour toute ma vie I'm your'n,' said she,
  ' I'm your regular little wife.'

' M'ami,' says he, ' I does these jobs
  In jocum—get up from your knees,
Would you offer outright to requite a knight?
  Mon garçon, *he* takes the fees !'"

                                —*J. A. M.*

The Polka.

"Qui nunc dancere vult modo,
Wants to dance in the fashion, oh !
Discere debit ought to know,
Kickere floor cum heel and toe.
    One, two, three
    Come hop with me—
Whirligig, twirligig, rapidee.

Polkam, jungere, Virgo vis?
Will you join in the polka, miss?
Liberius, most willingly,
Sic agemus, then let us try.
    Nunc vide,
    Skip with me.
Whirlabout, roundabout, celere.

Tum læva cito tum dextra,
First to the left, then t'other way ;
Aspice retro in vultu,
You look at her, she looks at you.
    Das palmam,
    Change hands, ma'am,
Celere, run away, just in sham."
          —*Gilbert Abbot A'Becket.*

Clubbis Noster.

"Sunt quidam jolly dogs, Saturday qui nocte frequentant,
Antiqui Stephanon, qui stat prope mœnia Drury,
Where they called for saccos cum prog distendere bellies,

F

Indulgere jocis, nec non Baccho atque tobacco ;
In mundo tales non fellows ante fuere
Magnanionam heroum celebrabe carmine laudeo,
Posthæ illustres ut vivant omne per ævum,
Altior en Stephano locus est, snug, cosy recessus,
Hic quarters fixere suos, conclave tenet hic,
Hic dapibus cumulata, hic mahogany mensa,
Pascuntur varies, roast beef cum pudding of Yorkshire,
Interdum, sometimes epulis quis nomen agrestes
Boiled leg of mutton and trimmings imposuere
Hic double X haurit, Barclay and Perkins ille.
Sic erimus drunki, Deel care ! aras dat mendicinum
Nec desuit mixtis que sese polibus implent.
Quus 'offnoff' omnes consuescunt dicere waiters.

    Postquam, exempta fames grubbo mappaque remota.
Pro cyathio clarmet, qui goes sermone vocantur.
Vulgari, of whiskey, rum, gin and brandy, sed ut sunt ;
Cœlicolumqui punch ('erroribus absque') liquore
Gaudent ; et panci vino quod prœbet Opporto,
Quod certi black-strap dicunt nicknomine Graii,
Haustibus his pipe, communis et adjiciuntur,
Shag, Reditus, Cubæ, Silvæ, Cheroots et Havanæ,
' Festina viri,' bawls one, 'nunc ludito verbis,'
Alter ' Fœmineum sexum ' propinquat et ' Hurrah !'
Respondet pot house concessu plausibus omni.
Nunc similes, veteri versantur winky lepores
Omnibus exiguus nec.   Jingoteste tumultus,
Exoritur quoniam summâ, nituntur opum vi
Rivales ἄλλοι top sawyers' ἐμμεναι ἀλλῶν,

Est genus injenui lusûs quod nomine Burking.
Notem est, vel Burko, qui claudere cuncta solebat
Ora olim, eloquio, pugili vel forsitan isto
Deaf un, vel Burko pueros qui Burxit ad illud,
Plausibus aut fictis joculatorem excipiendo,
Aut bothering aliquid referentem, constat amicum.
Hoc parvo excutitur multus conamine risus.
   Nomina magnorum referebam nunc pauca viorum,
Marcus et Henricus Punchi duo lumina magna
(Whacks his Aristoteleam, Sophoclem, Brown wollopeth
      ille)
In clubbum adveniunt, Juvenalis et advenit acer
Qui veluti Paddywhack for love conlundit amicos ;
Ingentesque animos non parvo in corpore versans
Tullius ; et Matutini qui Sidus Heraldi est
Georgius ; Albertus Magnus ; vesterque poeta.
Præsidet his Nestor qui tempore vixit in annæ,
Credetur et vidisse Jophet, non youngster at ullos.
In chaff, audaci certamine, vinceret illum,
Ille jocus mollit dictis, et pectora mulcet,
Ni faciat tumblers, et goes, et pocula pewter,
Quippe Aliorum alii jactarent forsan in aures."

                              —*Punch.*

LITTLE RED RIDING HOOD.

" You ask me to tell you the story
   Of the terrible atra wood,
Of the Lupi diri, μικρο παι,
   Και parvula Red Riding Hood.

Patruus trux, he gave her
   A deux larrons pravi ;
Et dear little robins came and
   Cut up cum the folii.

And then he scandit Beanstalk,
   And giant cædit tall
Et virgo grandis marri-ed
   Et Rem is prodegit all !

For, semble, une felis was left him —
   (Seulement, calamitas !)
Il emit chat zwei ocreæ
   Et was Marquis de Carrabas !

Καί ηει de lady et Ursus
  ・ (You've heard this much, at least),
Et fœmina on l'appèle Beauté,
   And the Beast they called A Beast !

Obdormivit, et amittit
   Ses moutons and couldn't find 'em,
So she never did nothing whatever at all,
   Et voila ! cum caudis behind 'em !

Comme des toutes les demoiselles charmantes
   Illæ the only lass
Who could yank her foot nitide
   Dans le pantoufle de glass !

Et straw she nevit in auribus,
   Et finally—child did win

De expiscere Arcanum name
  Nami erat Rumplestiltzskin !

Τρίχε ὅικαδε μίχρο ται :
  Ciel ! c'est time you should !
Ad lectum to dream of the story
  Of little Red Riding Hood !"

             —*J. A. M.*

      "Ich bin Dein."

" In tempus old a hero lived,
  Qui loved puellas deux ;
He ne pouvait pas quite to say
  Which one amabat mieux.

Dit-il lui-meme, un beau matin,
  ' Non possum both avoir,
Sed si address Amanda Ann,
  Then Kate and I have war.

' Amanda habet argent coin,
  Sed Kate has aureas curls :
Et both sunt very ἀγαθὰ,
  Et quite formosa girls.

Enfin, the youthful anthropos,
  Φιλοῦν the duo maids,
Resolved proponere ad Kate
  Devant cet evening's shades.

Procedens then to Kate's domo,
  Il trouve Amanda there ;

Καὶ quite forgot his good resolves,
　　Both sunt so goodly fair.

Sed, smiling on the new tapis,
　　Between puellas twain,
Cœpit to tell his flame to Kate
　　Dans un poetique strain.

Mais, glancing ever and anon
　　At fair Amanda's eyes,
Illæ non possunt dicere,
　　Pro which he meant his sighs.

Each virgo heard the demi vow
　　With cheeks as rouge as wine,
And offering each a milk-white hand,
　　Both whispered, ' Ich bin dein ! ' "

CONTENTI ABEAMUS.

" Come, jocund friends, a bottle bring,
　　And push around the jorum ;
We'll talk and laugh, and quaff and sing,
　　Nunc suavium amorum.

While we are in a merry mood,
　　Come, sit down ad bibendum ;
And if dull care should dare intrude,
　　We'll to the devil send him.

A moping elf I can't endure
　　While I have ready rhino ;
And all life's pleasures centre still
　　In venere ac vino.

Be merry then, my friends, I pray,
  And pass your time in joco,
For it is pleasant, as they say,
  Desipere in loco.

He that loves not a young lass,
  Is sure an arrant stultus,
And he that will not take a glass
  Deserves to be sepultus.

Pleasure, music, love and wine,
  Res valde sunt jocundæ,
And pretty maidens look divine,
  Provided ut sunt mundæ.

I hate a snarling, surly fool,
  Qui latrat sicut canis,
Who mopes and ever eats by rule,
  Drinks water and eats panis.

Give me the man that's always free,
  Qui finit molli more,
The cares of life, whate'er they be,
  Whose motto still is 'Spero.'

Death will turn us soon from hence,
  Nigerrimas ad sedes ;
And all our lands and all our pence
  Ditabunt tunc heredes.

Why should we then forbear to sport?
  Dum vivamus, vivamus,
And when the Fates shall cut us down,
  Contenti abeamus."

De Leguleio.

" Jurisconsultus juvenis solus,
　　Sat scanning his tenuem docket—
Volo, quoth he, some bonus Æolus
　　Inspiret fees to my pocket.

He seized in manua sinistra ejus
　　A tome of Noy, or Fortescue ;
Here's a case, said he, terrible tedious—
　　Fortuna veni to my rescue !

Lex scripta's nought but legal diluvium,
　　Defluxum streams of past ages,
And lawyers sit like ducks in a pluvium,
　　Under Law's reigning adages.

Lex non scripta's good for consciences tender,
　　Persequi the light internal ;
Sed homines sæpius homage render
　　Ad lucem that burns infernal.

Effodi the said diluvium over,
　　As do all legal beginners,
Et crede vivere hence in clover,
　　That's sown by quarrelsome sinners.

Some think the law esse hum scarabeum,
　　And lawyers a useless evil,
And Statute claim of tuum and meum
　　Is but a device of the devil ;

Sed pravi homines sunt so thick that,
  Without restrictio legis,
Esset crime plusquam one could shake stick at,
  By order diaboli regis.

Et good men, rari gurgite vasto,
  Are digni the law's assistance,
Defendere se, et aid them so as to
  Keep nefas et vim at a distance.

The lawyer's his client's rights' defender,
  And bound laborare astute,
Videre that quæquæ res agenda
  Dignitate et virtute.

Sed ecce ! a case exactly ad punctum—
  Id scribam, ante forget it,
Negotium illud nunc perfunctum,
  Feliciter, I have met it.

He thrust out dextræ digitos manus,
  His pennam ad ink ille dedit ;
Et scripsit,—but any homo sanus
  Would be nonsuit ere he could read it."

                —A. B. Ely.

CHANSON WITHOUT MUSIC.

BY THE PROFESSOR EMERITUS OF DEAD AND LIVING
LANGUAGES.

" You bid me sing—can I forget
  The classic odes of days gone by—
How belle Fifine and jeune Lisette
  Exclaimed, ' Anacreon γερὼν εἰ ? '

'Regardez donc,' those ladies said—
  'You're getting bald and wrinkled too :
When Summer's roses are all shed,
  Love's nullum ite, voyez vous !'

In vain ce brave Anacreon's cry,
  'Of love alone my banjo sings'
("Εϱῶτα μουνον).   'Etiam si,—
  Eh bien ?' replied those saucy things—
'Go find a maid whose hair is grey,
  And strike your lyre—we shan't complain ;
But parce nobis, s'il vous plait,—
  Voila Adolphe !   Voila Eugene !'

Ah, jeune Lisette ! ah, belle Fifine !
  Anacreon's lesson all must learn :
"Ο χαιϱός 'Οξὺς ; Spring is green,
  But acer Hiems waits his turn !
I hear you whispering from the dust,
  'Tiens, mon cher, c'est toujours so,—
The brightest blade grows dim with rust,
  The fairest meadow white with snow !'

You do not mean it ?   Not encore ?
  Another string of play-day rhymes ?
You've heard me—nonne est ?—before,
  Multoties,—more than twenty times ;
Non possum—vraiment—pas du tout,
  I cannot, I am loath to shirk ;
But who will listen if I do,
  My memory makes such shocking work ?

Γιγνώσκω. Scio. Yes, I'm told
    Some ancients like my rusty lay,
As Grandpa Noah loved the old
    Red-sandstone march of Jubal's day.
I used to carol like the birds,
    But time my wits have quite unfixed,
Et quoad verba—for my words—
    Ciel !—Eheu !—Whe-ew ! how they're mixed !

Mehercle ! Ζ.ϊ. Diable ! how
    My thoughts were dressed when I was young.
But tempus fugit—see them now
    Half clad in rags of every tongue !
O Φιλόι, fratres, chers amis !
    I dare not court the youthful muse,
For fear her sharp response should be—
    ' Papa Anacreon, please excuse ! '

Adieu ! I've trod my annual track
    How long !—let others count the miles—
And peddled out my rhyming pack
    To friends who always paid in smiles ;
So laissez moi ! some youthful wit
    No doubt has wares he wants to show,
And I am asking ' let me sit '
    Dum ille clamat " Δὸς ποῦ στῶ.' "

        —*Dr. Holmes, Atlantic Monthly, Nov.* 1867.

During the late American Civil War, Slidell and
Mason, two of the Confederate Commissioners, were

taken by an admiral of the U.S. navy from a British
ship, and this came near causing an issue between
the two countries.   Seward was the American pre-
mier at the time.   This is that affair done up in a
macaronic :

SLIDELL AND MASON.

"Slidell, qui est Rerum cantor
    Publicarum, atque Lincoln.
Vir excelsior, mitigantur—
    A delightful thing to think on !

Blatant plebs Americanum,
    Quite impossible to bridle,
Nihil refert, navis cana
    Bring back Mason atque Slidell.

Scribat nunc amœne Russell ;
    Lætus lapis claudit fiscum,
Nunc finiter all this bustle—
    Slidell—Mason—Pax vobiscum !"

A VALENTINE.

"Geist und sinn mich beutzen über
Vous zu dire das ich sie liebé ?
Das herz que vous so lightly spurn
To you und sie allein will turn
Unbarmherzig—pourquoir scorn
Mon cœur with love and anguish torn ;

Croyez vous das my despair
Votre bonheur can swell or faire?
Schönheit kann nicht cruel sein
Mefris ist kein macht divine,
Then, oh then, it can't be thine.
Glaube das mine love is true,
Changeless, deep wie Himmel's blue—
Que l'amour that now I swear,
Zue dir ewigkeit I'll bear
Glaube das de gentle rays,
Born and nourished in thy gaze,
Sur mon cœur will ever dwell
Comme à l'instant when they fell—
Mechante! that you know full well."

VERY FELIS-ITOUS.

" Felis sedit by a hole,
  Intente she, cum omni soul,
          Predere rats.
Mice cucurrerunt trans the floor,
In numero duo tres or more,
          Obliti cats.

Felis saw them oculis,
' I'll have them,' inquit she, ' I guess,
          Dum ludunt.'
Tunc illa crepit toward the group,
' Habeam,' dixit, ' good rat soup—
          Pingues sunt.'

Mice continued all ludere,
Intenti they in ludum vere,
  Gaudenter.
Tunc rushed the felis into them,
Et tore them omnes limb from limb,
  Violenter.

MORAL.

Mures omnes, nunc be shy,
Et aurem præbe mihi—
  Benigne :
Sic hoc satis—"verbum sat,"
Avoid a whopping Thomas cat
  Studiose."
    —*Green Kendrick.*

CE MÊME VIEUX COON.

"Ce meme vieux coon n'est pas quite mort,
 Il n'est pas seulement napping :
Je pense, myself, unless j'ai tort
 Cette chose est yet to happen.

En dix huit forty-four, je sais,
 Vous'll hear des curious noises ;
He'll whet ces dents against some Clay,
 Et scare des Loco—Bois-es !

You know que quand il est awake,
 Et quand il scratch ces clawses,
Les Locos dans leurs souliers shake,
 Et, sheepish, hang leurs jaws-es.

Ce meme vieux coon, je ne sais pas why,
  Le mischief's come across him,
Il fait believe he's going to die,
  Quand seulement playing possum.

Mais wait till nous le want encore,
  Nous'll stir him with une pole ;
He'll bite as mauvais as before
  Nous pulled him de son hole !"

—Relic of Henry Clay Campaign of 1844.

MALUM OPUS.

" Prope ripam fluvii solus
    A senex silently sat ;
Super capitem ecce his wig,
    Et wig super, ecce his hat.

Blew Zephyrus alte, acerbus,
    Dum elderly gentleman sat ;
Et a capite took up quite torve
    Et in rivum projecit his hat.

Tunc soft maledixit the old man,
    Tunc stooped from the bank where he sat,
Et cum scipio poked in the water,
    Conatus servare his hat.

Blew Zephyrus alte, acerbus,
    The moment it saw him at that ;
Et whisked his novum scratch wig
    In flumen, along with his hat.

Ab imo pectore damnavit
  In cœruleus eye dolor sat ;
Tunc despairingly threw in his cane
  Nare cum his wig and his hat.

L'ENVOI.

Contra bonos mores, don't swear,
  It est wicked, you know (verbum sat),
Si this tale habet no other moral,
  Mehercle ! you're gratus to that ! "

—*J. A. M.*

CARMEN AD TERRY.

(WRITTEN WHILE GENERAL TERRY, U.S.A., WITH HIS BLACK
SOLDIERS, WAS IN COMMAND AT RICHMOND, VIRGINIA, AFTER
ITS EVACUATION BY THE CONFEDERATE TROOPS.)

" Terry, leave us, sumus weary :
  Jam nos tædet te videre,
  Si vis nos with joy implere,
  Terry in hac terra tarry,
    Diem nary.

For thy domum long'st thou nonne ?
  Habes wife et filios bonny ?
  Socios Afros magis ton-y ?
  Haste thee, Terry, mili-terry,
    Pedem ferre.

Forte Thaddeus may desire thee,
  Sumner, et id. om., admire thee,
  Nuisance nobis, not to ire thee,

We can spare thee, magne Terry,
Freely, very.

Hear the Prex's proclamation,
Nos fideles to the nation,
Gone est nunc thy place and station
Terry-sier momen-terry
Sine query.

Yes, thy doom est scriptum—' Mene,'
Longer ne' nos naso tene,
Thou hast dogged us, diu bene,
Loose us, terrible bull terry-er,
We'll be merrier.

But the dulces Afros, vale,
Pompey, Scipio et Sally,
Seek some back New Haven alley,
Terry, quit this territory
Con amore.

Sed verbum titi, abituro,
Pay thy rent-bills, et conjuro,
Tecum take thy precious bureau
Terry, Turner, blue-coat hom'nes
Abhinc omnes ! "
—*Horace Milton.*

LYDIA GREEN.

" In Republican Jersey,
  There nunquam was seen
  Puella pulchrior,
  Ac Lydia Green ;

G

Fascinans quam bellis
Vel lilium, et id.,
Et Jacobus Brown
Was 'ladles'* on Lyd.

Ad Jacobum Brown
Semel Lydia, loquitur :
'Si fidem violaris,
I'd lay down and die, sir.'
'Si my Lydia dear
I should ever forget '—
Tum respondit : 'I hope
To be roasted and ate.'

Sed, though Jacob had sworn
Pro aris et focis,
He went off and left Lydia
Deserta, lachrymosis.
In lachrymis solvis
She sobbed and she sighed ;
And at last, corde fracta,
Turned over and died.

Tunc Jacobus Brown,
Se expedire pains
That gnawed his chords cordis,
Went out on the plains,
And quum he got there.
῎Οι Βάρβαροι met him,

---

* "Ladles "—*i.e.*, very spooney.

Accenderunt ignem
Et roasted et ate him."

—J. A. M.

AM RHEIN.

"Oh the Rhine, the Rhine, the Rhine—
  Comme c'est beau ! wie schön, che bello !
He who quaffs thy Lust and Wein,
  Morbleu ! is a lucky fellow.

How I love thy rushing streams,
  Groves and ash and birch and hazel,
From Schaffhausen's rainbow beams
  Jusqu'à l'echo d'Oberwesel !

Oh, que j'aime thy Brüchen, when
  The crammed Dampfschiff gaily passes !
Love the bronzed pipes of thy men,
  And the bronzed cheeks of thy lasses !

Oh ! que j'aime the ' oui,' the ' bah ! '
  From the motley crowd that flow,
With the universal ' ja,'
  And the Allgemeine ' so ! ' "

" SERVE-UM-RIGHT."

" ' Eh ! dancez-vous ? ' dixit Mein Herr.
  ' Oui, oui ! ' the charming maid replied :
Vidit ille at once the snare,
  Looked downas quick, et etiam sighed.

Das Mädchen knew each bona art
  Stat ludicrans superba sweet ;

Simplex homo perdit his heart
　　Declares eros ad ejus feet.

' Mein Liebchen,' here exclaims de Herr,
　　' Lux of mein life, ein rayum shed,
Dein oscula let amor share,
　　Si non, alas ! meum be dead.'

Ludit das girlus gaily then,
　　Cum scorna much upon her lip:
Quid stultuses sunt all you men,
　　Funus to give you omnes slip.

Mein Herr uprose cum dignas now,
　　Et melius et wiser man,
Der nubis paina on his brow,
　　To his dark domus cito ran.

Nunc omnes you qui eager hear
　　Meas tell of cette falsa maid,
Of fascinatus girl beware
　　Lest votre folly sic be paid."

To a Friend at Parting.

" I often wished I had a friend,
　Dem ich mich anvertraun Könnt,
A friend in whom I could confide,
　Der mit mir theilte Freud und Leid ;
Had I the riches of Girard—
　Ich theilte mit ihm Haus und Heerd :
For what is gold ?　'Tis but a passing metal,
　Der Henker hol' für mich den ganzen Bettel.

Could I purchase the world to live in it alone,
Ich gäb', däfur nich eine noble Bohn';
I thought one time in you I'd find that friend,
Und glaubte schon mein Sehnen hät ein End;
Alas! your friendship lasted but in sight,
Doch meine grenzet an die Ewigkeit."

AD PROFESSOREM LINGUÆ GERMANICÆ.

"Oh why now sprechen Sie Deutsch?
    What pleasure say can Sie haben?
You cannot imagine how much
    You bother unfortunate Knaben.

Liebster Freund! give bessere work,
    Nicht so hard, ein kurtzerer lesson,
Oh then we will nicht try to shirk
    Und unser will geben Sie blessin'.

Oh, ask us nicht now to decline
    'Meines Bruders grössere Häuser;'
'Die Fasser' of 'alt rother Wein'
    Can give us no possible joy, sir.

Der Müller may tragen ein Rock
    Eat schwartz Brod und dem Käse,
Die Gans may be hängen on hoch,
    But what can it matter to me, sir?

Return zu Ihr own native tongue,
    Leave Dutch und Sauer Kraut to the Dutchmen;
And seek not to teach to the young
    The Sprache belonging to such men.

Und now 'tis my solemn belief
  That if you nicht grant this petition,
Sie must schreiben mein Vater ein Brief,
  To say that ich hab' ein 'Condition.'"
                    — *Yale Courant.*

Pome of a Possum.

"The nox was lit by lux of Luna,
  And 'twas nox most opportuna
  To catch a possum or a coona ;
  For nix was scattered o'er this mundus,
  A shallow nix, et non profundus.
  On sic a nox with canis unus,
  Two boys went out to hunt for coonus.
        Unis canis, duo puer,
  Nunquam braver, nunquam truer,
  Quam hoc trio unquam fuit,
  If there was I never knew it.
  The corpus of this bonus canis,
  Was full as long as octo span is,
  But brevior legs had canis never
  Quam had hic dog ; et bonus clever
  Some used to say, in stultum jocum,
  Quod a field was too small locum
  For sic a dog to make a turnus
  Circum self from stem to sternus.
    This bonus dog had one bad habit,
  Amabat much to tree a rabbit—
  Amabat plus to chase a rattus,
  Amabat bene tree a cattus.

But on this nixy moonlight night,
This old canis did just right.
Nunquam treed a starving rattus,
Nunquam chased a starving cattus,
But cucurrit on, intentus
On the track and on the scentus,
Till he treed a possum strongum,
In a hollow trunkum longum ;
Loud he barked, in horrid bellum,
Seemed on terra venit pellum ;
Quickly ran the duo puer,
Mors of possum to secure ;
Quum venerit, one began
To chop away like quisque man ;
Soon the axe went through the truncum,
Soon he hit it all kerchunkum ;
Combat deepens ; on ye braves !
Canis, pueri et staves ;
As his powers non longuis tarry,
Possum potest non pugnare,
On the nix his corpus lieth,
Down to Hades spirit flieth,
Joyful pueri, canis bonus,
Think him dead as any stonus.

    Now they seek their pater's domo,
Feeling proud as any homo,
Knowing, certe, they will blossom
Into heroes, when with possum
They arrive, narrabunt story,
Plenus blood et plenior glory.

Pompey, David, Samson, Cæsar,
Cyrus, Blackhawk, Shalmaneser!
Tell me where est now the gloria,
Where the honours of Victoria?
　　Quum ad domum narrent story,
Plenus sanguine, tragic, gory.
Pater praiseth, likewise mater,
Wonders greatly younger frater.
Possum leave they on the mundus,
Go themselves to sleep profundus,
Somniunt possums slain in battle,
Strong as ursæ, large as cattle.

When nox gives way to lux of morning—
Albam terram much adorning,—
Up they jump to see the varmen,
Of the which this is the carmen.
Lo! possum est resurrectum!
Ecce pueri dejectum.
Ne relinquit track behind him,
Et the pueri never find him.
Cruel possum! bestia vilest,
How the pueros thou beguilest;
Pueri think non plus of Cæsar,
Go ad Orcum, Shalmaneser,
Take your laurels, cum the honour,
Since ista possum is a goner!"

The following "Society Verses" of Mortimer

Collins are given here by way of introducing an
imitation of them in macaronic verse :

AD CHLOEN, M.A.

(FRESH FROM HER CAMBRIDGE EXAMINATION.)

" Lady, very fair are you,
And your eyes are very blue,
  And your nose ;
And your brow is like the snow ;
And the various things you know
  Goodness knows.

And the rose-flush on your cheek,
And your Algebra and Greek
  Perfect are ;
And that loving lustrous eye
Recognises in the sky
  Every star.

You have pouting, piquant lips,
You can doubtless an eclipse
  Calculate ;
But for your cerulean hue,
I had certainly from you
  Met my fate.

If by an arrangement dual
I were Adams mixed with Whewell,
  The same day
I, as wooer, perhaps may come
To so sweet an Artium
  Magistra."

To the Fair "Come-Outer."

" Lady ! formosissima tu !
Cæruleis oculis have you,
        Ditto nose !
Et vous n'avez pas une faute—
And that you are going to vote,
        Goodness knows !

And the roseus on your cheek,
And your Algebra and Greek,
        Are parfait !
And your jactus oculi
Knows each star that shines in the
        Milky Way !

You have pouting, piquant lips,
Sans doute vous pouvez an eclipse
        Calculate !
Ne cærulum colorantur,
I should have in you, instanter,
        Met my fate !

Si, by some arrangement dual,
I at once were Kant and Whewell;
        It would pay—
Procus noti then to come
To so sweet an Artium
        Magistra !

Or, Jewel of Consistency,
Si possem clear-starch, cookere,
        Votre learning

Might the legēs proscribĕre —
Do the pro patria mori,
     I, the churning!"

Here are a few juvenile specimens, the first being
a little-known old nursery ballad:

THE FOUR BROTHERS.

" I had four brothers over the sea,
    Perrimerri dictum, Domine :
And each one sent a present to me ;
Partum quartum, peredecentum,
    Perrimerri dictum, Domine.

The first sent a cherry without any stone ;
    Perrimerri dictum, Domine :
The second a chicken without any bone,
Partum quartum, peredecentum,
    Perrimerri dictum, Domine.

The third sent a blanket without any thread ;
    Perrimerri dictum, Domine :
The fourth sent a book that no man could read ;
Partum quartum, peredecentum,
    Perrimerri dictum, Domine.

When the cherry's in the blossom, it has no stone ;
    Perrimerri dictum, Domine :
When the chicken's in the egg, it has no bone ;
Partum quartum, peredecentum,
    Perrimerri dictum, Domine.

When the blanket's in the fleece, it has no thread ;
  Perrimerri dictum, Domine :
When the book's in the press, no man can it read ;
Partum quartum, peredecentum,
  Perrimerri dictum, Domine."

LITTLE BO-PEEP.

" Parvula Bo-peep
  Amisit her sheep,
Et nescit where to find 'em ;
  Desere alone,
  Et venient home,
Cum omnibus caudis behind 'em."

JACK AND JILL.

" Jack cum amico Jill,
  Ascendit super montem ;
Johannes cecedit down the hill,
  Ex forte fregit frontem."

THE TEETOTUM.

" Fresh from his books, an arch but studious boy,
  Twirl'd with resilient glee his mobile toy ;
And while on single pivot foot it set,
Whisk'd round the board in whirring pirouette,
Shriek'd, as its figures flew too fast to note 'em,
Te totum amo, amo te, Teetotum."

Schoolboys and college youths not unfrequently
adorn their books with some such macaronic as
this :

" Si quisquis furetur,
  This little libellum,
Per Bacchum, per Jovem,
  I'll kill him, I'll fell him ;
In venturum illius
  I'll stick my scalpellum,
And teach him to steal
  My little libellum."

Inscriptions and epitaphs are often the vehicles of quaint and curious diction, and of these we give some instances :

THE SIGN OF THE "GENTLE SHEPHERD OF SALISBURY PLAIN."

On the road from Cape Town to Simon's Bay, Cape of Good Hope.)

" Multum in parvo, pro bono publico ;
Entertainment for man or beast all of a row.
Lekker host as much as you please ;
Excellent beds without any fleas ;
Nos patrum fugimus—now we are here,
Vivamus, let us live by selling beer
On donne à boire et á manger ici ;
Come in and try it, whoever you be."

IN THE VISITORS' BOOK AT NIAGARA FALLS.

" Tres fratres stolidii,
Took a boat at Niagri ;
Stormus arose et windus erat,
Magnum frothum surgebat,
Et boatum overturnebat,
Et omnes drowndiderunt
Quia swimmere non potuerunt ! "

IN THE VISITORS' BOOK OF MOUNT KEARSARGE HOUSE.

(Summit of Mount Kearsarge, North Conway, N.H.)

" Sic itur ad astra, together ;
But much as we aspire,

No purse of gold, this summer weather,
Could hire us to go higher ! "

The following epitaph is to be found in North-
allerton Churchyard:

" Hic jacet Walter Gun,
    Sometime landlord of the *Sun*,
Sic transit gloria mundi !
    He drank hard upon Friday,
    That being an high day,
Took his bed and died upon Sunday ! "

There are no macaronic authors nowadays,
though poems of this class are still to be had in
colleges and universities; but everything pertain-
ing to college life is ephemeral, coming in with
Freshman and going out with Senior. College
students are the prolific fathers of a kind of
punning Latin composition, such as:

" O *unum* sculls. You *damnum* sculls. *Sic transit*
drove a *tu pone tandem temo ver* from the north."

" He is visiting his *ante*, Mrs. *Dido Etdux*, and intends
stopping here till *ortum*."

" He *et super* with us last evening, and is a terrible
fellow.   He *lambda* man almost to death the other
evening, but he got his match—the other man *cutis nos*
off for him and *noctem* flat *urna* flounder."

" Doctores !   Ducum nex mundi nitu Panes; tritucum
at ait.   Expecto meta fumen, and eta beta pi.   Super

attente one—Dux, hamor clam pati ; sum parates, homine, ices, jam, etc.   Sideror hoc."

In a similar dialect to this, Dean Swift and Dr. Sheridan used to correspond.   In this way :

"Is his honor sic ?   Præ letus felis pulse."

The Dean once wrote to the Doctor :

"Mollis abuti,   No lasso finis,
 Has an acuti,   Molli divinis."

To which the Doctor responded :

"I ritu a verse o na Molli o mi ne,
Asta lassa me pole, a lædis o fine ;
I ne ver neu a niso ne at in mi ni is,
A manat a glans ora sito fer diis.

De armo lis abuti, hos face an hos nos is
As fer a sal illi, as reddas aro sis,
Ac is o mi Molli is almi de lite,
Illo verbi de, an illo verbi nite."

At this the Dean settles the whole affair by—

"Apud in is almi de si re,
  Mimis tres I ne ver re qui re ;
  Alo' ver I findit a gestis,
  His miseri ne ver at restis."

Sydney Smith proposed as a motto for a well-known fish-sauce purveyor the following line from Virgil (*Æn.* iv. 1):

"*Gravi jam*dudum *saucia* curâ."

When two students named Payne and Culpepper were expelled from college, a classmate wrote :

"*Pœn*ia perire potest ; *Culpa pere*nnis est."

And Dr. Johnson wrote the following epitaph on his cat :

"*Mi-cat* inter omnes."

A gentleman at dinner helped his friend to a potato, saying—"I think that is a good mealy one." "Thank you," was the reply, "it could not be *melior*."

Another gentleman while driving one day was asked by a lady if some fowls they passed were ducks or geese. One of the latter at the moment lifting up its voice, the gentleman said, "That's your *anser !*"

"Well, Tom, are you sick again?" asked a student of his friend, and was answered in English and in Latin, "*Sic sum.*"

Victor Hugo was once asked if he could write English poetry. "Certainement," was the reply, and he sat down and wrote this verse :

"Pour chasser le spleen
J'entrai dans un inn ;
O, mais je bus le gin,
God save the queen !"

In the "Innocents Abroad" of Mark Twain he gives a letter written by his friend Mr. Blucher to a Parisian hotel-keeper, which was as follows :

"'MONSIEUR LE LANDLORD : Sir—*Pourquoi* don't you

mettez some *savon* in your bed-chambers? *Est-ce-que-
vous pensez* I will steal it? *Le nuit passeé* you charged
me *pour deux chandelles* when I only had one; *hier vous
avez* charged me *avec glace* when I had none at all; *tout
les jours* you are coming some fresh game or other upon
me, *mais vous ne pouvez pas* play this *savon* dodge on me
twice. *Savon* is a necessary *de la vie* to anybody but a
Frenchman, *et je l'aurai hors de cette hotel* or make trouble.
You hear me.—*Allons.*   BLUCHER.'

"I remonstrated," says Mr. Twain, "against the
sending of this note, because it was so mixed up
that the landlord would never be able to make
head or tail of it; but Blucher said he guessed the
old man could read the French of it, and average
the rest."

Productions like the preceding, and like that
with which we conclude are continually finding
their way into print, and are always readable, curious, and fresh for an idle hour.

POCAHONTAS AND CAPTAIN SMITH.

(JAMESTOWN, A.D. 1607.)

"Johannes Smithus, walking up a streetus, met two
ingentes Ingins et parvulus Ingin. Ingins non capti
sunt ab Johanne, sed Johannes captus est ab ingentibus
Inginibus. Parvulus Ingin run off hollerin, et terriffi-
ficatus est most to death. Big Ingin removit Johannem

H

ad tentem, ad campum, ad marshy placem, papoosem, pipe of peacem, bogibus, squawque. Quum Johannes examinatus est ab Inginibus, they condemnati sunt eum to be cracked on capitem ab clubbibus. Et a big Ingin was going to strikaturus esse Smithum with a clubbe, quum Pocahontas came trembling down, et hollerin, ' Don't ye duit, don't ye duit ! ' Sic Johannes non periit, sed grew fat on corn bread et hominy."

NE of the most curious efforts in the way of teaching a language was that attempted by a work published originally in Paris, in 1862, entitled "O Novo Guia em Portuguez e Inglez. Par Jose de Fonseca e Pedro Carolina," or the New Guide to Conversation in Portuguese and English. Mr. G. C. Leland writes us that Fonseca "manufactured" this work by procuring a book of French dialogues, which he put word by word into English "—(by the aid of a dictionary)—"of which he knew not a word, and what is strangest, did not learn a word, even while writing his *Guide.* That he really humbugged his bookseller appears from this that he induced the poor victim to publish a large English dictionary!" This book has been reprinted, as a literary curiosity, and may be had at Quaritch's, 15 Piccadilly, London, under the title of "A New Guide to the English," by Pedro Carolina; Fonseca having taken his name out, and dating the book from "Pekin," —this being a mere joke. However, the original was a serious work, and by way of introduction to a poem in the Fonseca English, kindly given us by Professor E. H. Palmer, we give a few particulars of and extracts from the work itself, and here is the Preface :

"A choice of familiar dialogues, clean of gallicisms and despoiled phrases, it was missing yet to studious portuguese and brazilian Youth ; and also to persons of other nations that wish to know the portuguese language. We sought all we may do, to correct that want, composing and divising the present little work in two parts. The first includes a greatest vocabulary proper names by alphabetical order ; and the second forty-three Dialogues adapted to the usual precisions of the life. For that reason we did put, with a scrupulous exactness, a great variety own expressions to english and portugues idioms ; without to attach us selves (as make some others) almost at a literal translation ; translation what only will be for to accustom the portuguese pupils, or-foreign, to speak very bad any of the mentioned idioms. We were increasing this second edition with a phraseology, in the first part, and some familiar letters, anecdotes, idiotisms, proverbs, and to second a coin's index.

"The *Works* which we were confering for this labour, find use us for nothing ; but those what were publishing to Portugal, or out. They were almost all composed for some foreign, or for some national little acquainted in the spirit of both languages. It was resulting from that corelessness to rest these *Works* fill of imperfections and anomalies of style; in spite of the infinite typographical faults which sometimes invert the sense of the periods. It increase not to contain any of those *Works* the figured pronunciation of the english words, nor the prosodical accent in the portugese : indispensable object whom wish to speak the english and portuguese languages correctly.

"We expect then who the little book (for the care what we wrote him, and for her typographical correction) that may be worth the acceptance of the studious persons, and especially of the Youth, at which we dedicate him particularly."

The "greatest vocabulary proper names" is in three columns—the first giving the Portuguese, the second the English words, and the third the English pronunciation :

Dô Múndo.	Of the world.	Ove thi Ueurlde.
Os astros.	The stars.	Thi esters.
Môça.	Young girl.	Yeun-gue guerle.
O relâmpago.	The flash of lightning.	Thi flax ove lait eningue.

The vocabulary fills about fifty pages, and is followed by a series of " familiar phrases," of which a few are here given :

"Do which is that book? Do is so kind to tell me it. Let us go on ours feet. Having take my leave, i was going. This trees make a beauty shade. This wood is full of thiefs. These apricots make me & to come water in mouth. I have not stricken the clock. The storm is go over, the sun begin to dissape it. I am stronger which him. That place is too much gracious. That are the dishes whose you must be and to abstain."

Then come the dialogues, and one we give is supposed to take place at a morning call, which commences first with the visitor and the servant:

"'Is your master at home?'—'Yes, sir.' 'Is it up?'— 'No, sir, he sleep yet. I go make that he get up.' 'It come in one's? How is it you are in bed yet?'— 'Yesterday at evening I was to bed so late that i may not rising me soon that morning.'"

This is followed by a description of the dissipation which led to these late hours—"singing, dancing, laughing, and playing"—

"'What game?'—'To the picket.' 'Who have prevailed upon?'—'I have gained ten lewis.' 'Till at what o'clock its had play one?'—'Untill two o'clock after midnight.'"

But these conversations or dialogues, however amusing, are as nothing when compared with the anecdotes which are given by Fonseca, of which we transcribe a few:

"John II. Portugal King, had taken his party immediately. He had in her court castillians ambassadors coming for treat of the pease. As they had keeped in leng the negotiation he did them two papers in one from which he had wrote *peace* and on the other *war*—telling them 'Choice you !'"

"Philip, King's Macedonia, being fall, and seeing the extension of her body drawed upon the dust was cry —'Greats Gods ! that we may have little part in this Univers !'"

"One eyed was laied against a man which had good eyes that he saw better than him. The party was accepted. 'I had gain over,' said the one eyed; 'why i see you two eyes, and you not look me who one !'"

"The most vertious of the pagans, Socrates, was accused from impiety, and immolated to the fury of the envy and the fanaticism. When relates one's him self that he has been condemned to death for the Athenians —'And then told him, they are it for the nature,—But it is an unjustly,' cried her woman 'would thy replied-him that might be justify?'"

"Cæsar seeing one day to Roma, some strangers, very riches, which bore between her arms little dogs and little monkeies and who was carressign them too tenderly was ask, with so many great deal reason, whether the women of her country don't had some children?"

"Two friends who from long they not were seen meet one's selves for hazard. 'How do is there?' told one of the two. 'No very well, told the other, and i am married from that I saw thee.' 'Good news.' 'Not quit, because

I had married with a bad woman.' 'So much worse.'
'Not so much great deal worse; because her dower was
from two thousand lewis.' 'Well, that confort.' 'Not
absolutely, why i had emplored this sum for to buy some
muttons which are all deads of the rot.' 'That is indeed
very sorry.' 'Not so sorry, because the selling of hers
hide have bring me above the price of the muttons.'
'So you are indemnified.' 'Not quit, because my house
where i was disposed my money, finish to be consumed
by the flames.' 'Oh, here is a great misfortune!'
'Not so great nor i either, because my wife and my
house are burned together!'"

The concluding portion of this Guide is devoted
to "Idiotisms and Proverbs," of some of which it
is rather difficult to recognise the original, as "To
take time by the forelock," is rendered "It want
to take the occasion for the hairs!" Here are a
few others :

"The walls have hearsay."
"Four eyes does see better than two."
"There is not any ruler without a exception."
"The mountain in work put out a mouse."
"He is like the fish into the water."
"To buy a cat in a pocket."
"To come back at their muttons."
"He is not so devil as he is black."
"Keep the chestnut of the fire with the hand of the cat."
"What come in to me for an ear yet out for another."

" Take out the live coals with the hand of the cat."
" These roses do button at the eyesight."

Enough perhaps has been given about this amusing Guide, and we here introduce Professor E. H. Palmer's verses:

THE PARTERRE.

A POETRY AS THE FONSECA.

" I don't know any greatest treat
    As sit him in a gay parterre,
And sniff one up the perfume sweet
    Of every roses buttoning there.

It only want my charming miss
    Who make to blush the self red rose ;
Oh ! I have envy of to kiss
    The end's tip of her splendid nose.

Oh ! I have envy of to be
    What grass neath her pantoffle push,
And too much happy seemeth me
    The margaret which her vestige crush.

But I will meet her nose at nose,
    And take occasion for the hairs,
And indicate her all my woes,
    That she in fine agree my prayers.

THE ENVOY.

I don't know any greatest treat
    As sit him in a gay parterre,

> With Madame who is too more sweet
> Than every roses buttoning there."

Pidgin English is the name given to the dialect extensively used in the seaport towns of China as a means of communication between the natives and English and Americans, and is a very rude jargon in which English words are very strangely distorted. It is very limited, the Chinese learning Pidgin with only the acquirement of a few hundred words, the pronunciation and grammar of which have been modified to suit those of their own language. The word Pidgin itself is derived through a series of changes in the word *Business.* Early traders made constant use of this word, and the Chinaman contracted it first to *Busin*, and then through the change to *Pishin* it at length assumed the form of *Pidgin*, still retaining its original meaning. This at once shows the difficulty which a Chinaman has in mastering the pronunciation of English words, and as business or commerce is the great bond of union between the Chinese and the foreign residents, it is not to be wondered at that this word should give name to the jargon formed in its service. The Chinese have great difficulty in using the letter *r*, pronouncing it almost always like *l*, as *loom* for *room*, *cly* for *cry;* and for the sake of euphony often add *ee* or *lo* to the end of words. *Galaw* or *galow* is a word of no meaning, being used as a kind of interjection ; *chop, chop,* means quick, quick ; *maskee,* don't mind ; *chop b'long,* of a kind ; *topside galow,* excelsior, or "hurrah for topside"; *chin chin,* good-bye; *welly culio,* very curious ; *Joss-pidgin-man,* priest. With these few hints the reader may understand better the following version of "Excelsior," which originally appeared in *Harpers' Magazine* in 1869,—the moral, however, belongs solely to the Chinese translator :

TOPSIDE-GALOW.

"That nightee teem he come chop chop
  One young man walkee, no can stop ;
  Colo maskee, icee maskee ;
  He got flag ; chop b'long we*ll*y cu*l*io, see—
               Topside-galow !

He too muchee so*ll*y ; one piecee eye
Looksee sharp—so fashion—alla same my :
He talkee largee, talkee st*l*ong,
Too muchee cu*l*io ; alla same gong—
               Topside-galow !

Inside any housee he can see light,
Any piecee *l*oom got fire all *l*ight ;
He looksee plenty ice more high,
Inside he mouf he plenty c*l*y—
               Topside-galow !

'No can walkee!' olo man speakee he;
'Bimeby *l*ain come, no can see;
Hab got water we*ll*y wide!'
Maskee, my must go topside—

     Topside-galow!

'Man-man,' one galo talkee he;
'What for you go topside look-see?'
'Nother teem,' he makee plenty c*l*y,
Maskee, alla teem walkee plenty high—

     Topside-galow!

'Take care that spilum t*l*ee, young man,
Take care that icee!' he no man-man,
That coolie chin-chin he 'Good-night;'
He talkee, 'My can go all *l*ight'—

     Topside-galow!

Joss-pidgin-man chop chop begin,
Morning teem that Joss chin-chin,
No see any man, he plenty fear,
Cause some man talkee, he can hear—

     Topside-galow!

Young man makee die; one largee dog see
Too muchee bobbe*l*y, findee hee.
Hand too muchee colo, inside can stop
Alla same piecee flag, got cu*l*io chop—

     Topside-galow!

MORAL.

You too muchee laugh! What for sing?
I think so you no savey t'hat ting!

Supposey you no b'long clever inside,
More betta *you* go walk topside !
                    Topside-galow ! "

In connection with these linguistic curiosities we take the following from an old number of *Harpers' Magazine :* "A practical parent objects to the silliness of our nursery rhymes, for the reason that the doggerel is rendered pernicious by the absence of a practical moral purpose, and as introducing infants to the realities of life through an utterly erroneous medium. They are taught to believe in a world peopled by Little Bo-peeps and Goosey, Goosey Ganders, instead of a world of New York Central, Erie, North-Western Preferred, &c. &c. It is proposed, therefore, to accommodate the teaching of the nursery to the requirements of the age, to invest children's rhymes with a moral purpose. Instead, for example, of the blind wonderment as to the nature of astronomical bodies inculcated in that feeble poem commencing ' Twinkle, twinkle, little star,' let the child be indoctrinated into the recent investigations of science, thus :

' Wrinkles, wrinkles, solar star,
    I obtain of what you are,
    When unto the noonday sky
    I the spectroscope apply ;

For the spectrum renders clear
Gaps within your photosphere,
Also sodium in the bar
Which your rays yield, solar star.'

" Then, again, there is the gastronomic career of
Little Jack Horner, which inculcates gluttony. It
is practicable that this fictitious hero should fami-
liarise the child with the principles of the *Delectus :*

'Studious John Horner,
Of Latin no scorner,
In the second declension did spy
How nouns there are some
Which ending in *um*
Do *not* make their plural in *i*.'

" The episode of Jack and Jill is valueless as an
educational medium. But it might be made to
illustrate the arguments of a certain school of political economists:

' Jack and Jill
Have studied Mill,
And all that sage has taught, too.
Now both promote
Jill's claim to vote,
As every good girl ought too.'

" Even the pleasures of life have their duties,
and the child needs to be instructed in the polite
relaxation of society. The unmeaning jingle of

'Hey diddle diddle,' might be invested with some utility of a social kind :

> ' I did an idyl on Joachim's fiddle,
>   At a classical soiree in June,
>   While jolly dogs laughed at themes from Spöhr,
>   And longed for a popular tune.'

"And the importance of securing a good *parti*, of rejecting ineligible candidates, and of modifying flirtations by a strict regard to the future, might be impressed upon the female mind at an early age in the following moral :

> ' Little Miss Muffit
>   Sat at a buffet
>   Eating a *bonbon sucre ;*
>   A younger son spied her,
>   And edged up beside her,
>   But she properly frowned him away.' "

The preceding is all very well, but there are others which have been travestied and changed also—"Mary's little Lamb," for instance, will never be allowed to rest in its true Saxon garb, but is being constantly dressed in every tongue and dialect.   But recently one has arisen bold enough to doubt the story altogether, and throw discredit on the song.   Mr. Baring Gould, and iconoclasts like him, strive to show that William Tell and other

ancient heroes never did live, but we never expected
to doubt the existence of "Mary's little Lamb," yet
a correspondent to a magazine sent not long ago
what he says is the "true story of Mary and her
lamb," hoping it will take the place of the garbled
version hitherto received as authentic:

> " Mary had a little lamb,
>   Whose fleece was white as snow,
>   And every place that Mary went,
>   The lamb it would *not* go.
>
>   So Mary took that little lamb,
>   And beat it for a spell ;
>   The family had it fried next day,
>   And it went very well."

We have still another way of it, in what may be
termed an exaggerated synonymic adherence to
the central idea of the ballad :

" Mary possessed a diminutive sheep,
  Whose external covering was as devoid of colour as
        the aqueous fluid which sometimes presents un-
        surmountable barriers on the Sierras.
  And everywhere Mary peregrinated
  This juvenile Southdown would be sure to get up and
    ·   go right after her.
  It followed her to the alphabet dispensary one day,
  Which was contrary to the 243d subdivision of the

714th article of the constitution of that academy of erudition ;

It caused the adolescent disciples there assembled to titillate their risibles and indulge in interludes of sportive hilarity," &c. &c.

Linguistic renderings of many of these ancient songs may be found in the works of the Rev. Francis Mahoney (Father Prout), Dr. Maginn, &c., as well as in the "Arundines Cami" of the Rev. H. Drury. Of these here follow a few:

LITTLE BO-PEEP.

" Petit Bo-peep
A perdu ses moutons
Et ne sait pas que les a pris,
O laisses les tranquilles
Ill viendront en ville
Et chacun sa que apres lui."

BA, BA, BLACK SHEEP.

" Ba, ba, mouton noir,
Avez vous de laine?
Oui Monsieur, non Monsieur,
Trois sacs pleine.
Un pour mon maitre, un pour ma dame,
Pas un pour le jeune enfant que pleure dan le chemin."

Here is a song of Mahoney's, which is given complete:

" Quam pulchra sunt ova
  Cum alba et nova,
In stabulo scite leguntur ;
  Et a Margery bella,
  Quæ festiva puella !
Pinguis lardi cum frustris coquuntur.

  Ut belles in prato,
  Aprico et lato
Sub sole tam lacte renident ;
  Ova tosta in mensa
  Mappa bene extensa,
Nittidissima lanse consident."

Which, put into English, is :

" Oh ! 'tis eggs are a treat,
  When so white and so sweet
From under the manger they're taken ;
  And by fair Margery
  (Och ! 'tis she's full of glee !)
They are fried with fat rashers of bacon.

  Just like daisies all spread,
  O'er a broad sunny mead,
In the sunbeams so gaudily shining,
  Are fried eggs, when displayed
  On a dish, when we've laid
The cloth, and are thinking of dining !"

The last of these we give is from the " Arundines Cami " :

TWINKLE, TWINKLE, LITTLE STAR.

" Mica, mica, parva Stella,
  Miror, quænam sis tam bella !
  Splendens eminus in illo
  Alba velut gemma, cœlo."

This familiar nursery rhyme has also been "revised" by a committee of eminent preceptors and scholars, with this result :

" Shine with irregular, intermitted light, sparkle at intervals,
    diminutive, luminous, heavenly body.
  How I conjecture, with surprise, not unmixed with uncer-
    tainty, what you are,
  Located, apparently, at such a remote distance from, and
    at a height so vastly superior to this earth, the planet
    we inhabit,
  Similar in general appearance and refractory powers to
    the precious primitive octahedron crystal of pure car-
    bon, set in the aërial region surrounding the earth."

Dr. Lang, in his book on " Queensland," &c., is wroth against the colonists for the system of nomenclature they have pursued, in so far as introducing such names as Deptford, Codrington, Greenwich, and so on. Conceding that there may be some confusion by the duplication in this way of names from the old country, they are surely better than the jaw-breaking native names which are strung together in the following lines :

" I like the native names, as Parramatta,
    And Illawarra and Wooloomooloo,
    Tongabbee, Mittagong, and Coolingatta,
    Eurauania, Jackwa, Bulkomatta,
    Nandowra, Tumbwumba, Woogaroo ;
    The Wollondilly and the Wingycarribbeo,
    The Warragumby, Dalby, and Bungarribbe."

The following *jeu d'esprit*, in which many of the
absurd and unpronounceable names of American
towns and villages are happily hit off, is from the
Orpheus C. Kerr (office-seeker) *Papers*, by R. H.
Newell, a work containing many of those humorous, semi-political effusions, which were so common
in the United States during the Civil War :

THE AMERICAN TRAVELLER.

" To Lake Aghmoogenegamook,
    All in the State of Maine,
A man from Wittequergaugaum came
    One evening in the rain.

' I am a traveller,' said he,
    ' Just started on a tour,
And go to Nomjamskillicook
    To-morrow morn at four.'

He took a tavern-bed that night,
    And with the morrow's sun,
By way of Sekledobskus went,
    With carpet-bag and gun.

A week passed on ; and next we find
  Our native tourist come
To that sequester'd village called
  Genasagarnagum.

From thence he went to Absequoit,
  And there—quite tired of Maine—
He sought the mountains of Vermont,
  Upon a railroad train.

Dog Hollow, in the Green Mount State,
  Was his first stopping-place,
And then Skunk's Misery displayed
  Its sweetness and its grace.

By easy stages then he went
  To visit Devil's Den ;
And Scrabble Hollow, by the way,
  Did come within his ken.

Then *via* Nine Holes and Goose Green,
  He travelled through the State,
And to Virginia, finally,
  Was guided by his fate.

Within the Old Dominion's bounds,
  He wandered up and down ;
To-day at Buzzard Roost ensconced,
  To-morrow at Hell Town.

At Pole Cat, too, he spent a week,
  Till friends from Bull Ring came,
And made him spend the day with them
  In hunting forest game.

Then, with his carpet-bag in hand,
　　To Dog Town next he went;
Though stopping at Free Negro Town,
　　Where half a day he spent.

From thence, into Negationburg
　　His route of travel lay,
Which having gained, he left the State
　　And took a southward way.

North Carolina's friendly soil
　　He trod at fall of night,
And, on a bed of softest down,
　　He slept at Hell's Delight.

Morn found him on the road again,
　　To Lousy Level bound ;
At Bull's Tail, and Lick Lizard too,
　　Good provender he found.

The country all about Pinch Gut
　　So beautiful did seem,
That the beholder thought it like
　　A picture in a dream.

But the plantations near Burnt Coat
　　Were even finer still,
And made the wond'ring tourist feel
　　A soft delicious thrill.

At Tear Shirt, too, the scenery
　　Most charming did appear,
With Snatch It in the distance far,
　　And Purgatory near.

But spite of all these pleasant scenes,
  The tourist stoutly swore
That home is brightest after all,
  And travel is a bore.

So back he went to Maine, straightway
  A little wife he took ;
And now is making nutmegs at
  Moosehicmagunticook."

A Rhyme for Musicians.

" Haendel, Bendel, Mendelssohn,
  Brendel, Wendel, Jadasshon,
  Muller, Hiller, Heller, Franz,
  Blothow, Flotow, Burto, Gantz.

Meyer, Geyer, Meyerbeer,
  Heyer, Weyer, Beyer, Beer,
  Lichner, Lachnar, Schachner, Dietz,
  Hill, Will, Bruell, Grill Drill, Reiss, Reitz.

Hansen, Jansen, Jensen, Kiehl,
  Siade, Gade, Laade, Stiehl,
  Naumann, Riemann, Diener, Wurst,
  Niemann, Kiemann, Diener Wurst.

Kochler, Dochler, Rubenstein,
  Himmel, Hummel, Rosenkyn,
  Lauer, Bauer, Kleincke,
  Homberg, Plomberg, Reinecke."

                              —*E. Lemke.*

SURNAMES.

BY JAMES SMITH, ONE OF THE AUTHORS OF "REJECTED ADDRESSES."

" Men once were surnamed for their shape or estate
    (You all may from history learn it),
There was Louis the Bulky, and Henry the Great,
    John Lackland, and Peter the Hermit.
But now, when the doorplates of misters and dames
    Are read, each so constantly varies ;
From the owner's trade, figure, and calling, surnames
    Seem given by the rule of contraries.

Mr. Wise is a dunce, Mr. King is a whig,
    Mr. Coffin's uncommonly sprightly,
And huge Mr. Little broke down in a gig,
    While driving fat Mrs. Golightly.
At Bath, where the feeble go more than the stout,
    (A conduct well worthy of Nero,)
Over poor Mr. Lightfoot, confined with the gout,
    Mr. Heavyside danced a bolero.

Miss Joy, wretched maid, when she chose Mr. Love,
    Found nothing but sorrow await her ;
She now holds in wedlock, as true as a dove,
    That fondest of mates, Mr. Hayter.
Mr. Oldcastle dwells in a modern-built hut ;
    Miss Sage is of madcaps the archest ;
Of all the queer bachelors Cupid e'er cut,
    Old Mr. Younghusband's the starchest.

Mr. Child, in a passion, knock'd down Mr. Rock ;
　Mr. Stone like an aspen-leaf shivers ;
Miss Pool used to dance, but she stands like a stock
　Ever since she became Mrs. Rivers.
Mr. Swift hobbles onward, no mortal knows how,
　He moves as though cords had entwined him ;
Mr. Metcalf ran off upon meeting a cow,
　With pale Mr. Turnbull behind him.

Mr. Barker's as mute as a fish in the sea,
　Mr. Miles never moves on a journey,
Mr. Gotobed sits up till half after three,
　Mr. Makepeace was bred an attorney.
Mr. Gardener can't tell a flower from a root,
　Mr. Wild with timidity draws back ;
Mr. Ryder performs all his journeys on foot,
　Mr. Foot all his journeys on horseback.

Mr. Penny, whose father was rolling in wealth,
　Consumed all the fortune his dad won ;
Large Mr. Le Fever's the picture of health ;
　Mr. Goodenough is but a bad one.
Mr. Cruikshank stept into three thousand a year
　By showing his leg to an heiress :
Now I hope you'll acknowledge I've made it quite clear
　Surnames ever go by contraries."

The next verses are somewhat similar, and are
taken from an old number of the *European
Magazine :*

COINCIDENCES AND CONTRARIETIES.

"'Tis curious to find, in this overgrown town,
   While through its long streets we are dodging,
That many a man is in trade settled down,
   Whose name don't agree with his lodging!
For instance, Jack Munday in Friday Street dwells,
   Mr. Pitt in Fox Court is residing;
Mr. White in Black's Buildings green-grocery sells,
   While East in West Square is abiding!

Mr. Lamb in Red Lion Street perks up his head,
   To Lamb's, Conduit Street, Lyon goes courting;
Mr. Boxer at Battle Bridge hires a bed,
   While Moon is in Sun Street disporting.
Bill Brown up to Green Street to live now is gone,
   In Stanhope mews Dennet keeps horses;
Doctor Low lives in High Street, Saint Mary-le-Bone,
   In Brown Street one Johnny White's door sees.

But still much more curious it is, when the streets
   Accord with the names of their tenants;
And yet with such curious accordance one meets,
   In taking a town-tour like Pennant's.
For instance, in Crown Street George King you may
      note,
   To Booth, in Mayfair, you go shopping;
And Porter, of Brewer Street, goes in a boat
   To Waters, of River Street, Wapping!

Mr. Sparrow in Bird Street has feathered his nest,
   Mr. Archer in Bow Street wooes Sally:

Mr. Windham in Air Street gets zephyr'd to rest,
   Mr. Dancer resides in Ball Alley.
Mr. Fisher on Finsbury fixes his views,
   Mrs. Foote in Shoe Lane works at carding ;
Mr. Hawke has a residence close to the Mews,
   And Winter puts up at Spring Gardens !

In Orange Street, Lemon vends porter and ale,
   In Hart Street, Jack Deer keeps a stable ;
In Hill Street located you'll find Mr. Dale,
   In Blue Anchor Row, Mr. Cable.
In Knight-Rider Street, you've both Walker and Day,
   In Castle Street, Champion and Spearman ;
In Blackman Street, Lillywhite makes a display,
   In Cheapside lives sweet Mrs. Dearman.

In Paradise Row, Mr. Adam sells figs,
   Eve, in Apple Tree Yard, rooms has taken ;
Mr. Coltman, in Foley Street, fits you with wigs,
   In Hog Lane you call upon Bacon.
Old Homer in Greek Street sells barrels and staves,
   While Pope, in Cross Lane, is a baker ;
In Liquorpond Street, Mr. Drinkwater shaves,
   In Cow Lane lives A. Veal, undertaker."

THE ENGLISH LANGUAGE.

" A pretty deer is dear to me,
   A hare with downy hair ;
I love a hart with all my heart,
   But barely bear a bear.
'Tis plain that no one takes a plane
   To pare a pair of pears ;

A rake, though, often takes a rake
　　To tear away the tares.
All rays raise thyme, time razes all ;
　　And, through the whole, hole wears.
A writ, in writing 'right,' may write
　　It 'wright,' and still be wrong—
For 'wright' and 'rite' are neither 'right,'
　　And don't to 'write' belong.
Beer often brings a bier to man,
　　Coughing a coffin brings ;
And too much ale will make us ail,
　　As well as other things.
The person lies who says he lies
　　When he is but reclining ;
And when consumptive folks decline,
　　They all decline declining.
A quail don't quail before a storm—
　　A bough will bow before it ;
We cannot rein the rain at all—
　　No earthly powers reign o'er it ;
The dyer dyes awhile, then dies ;
　　To dye he's always trying,
Until upon his dying bed
　　He thinks no more of dyeing.
A son of Mars mars many a sun ;
　　All deys must have their days,
And every knight should pray each night
　　To Him who weighs his ways.
'Tis meet that man should mete out meat
　　To feed misfortune's son ;

The fair should fare on love alone,
  Else one cannot be won.
A lass, alas! is something false ;
  Of faults a maid is made ;
Her waist is but a barren waste—
  Though stayed she is not staid.
The springs spring forth in spring, and shoots
  Shoot forward one and all ;
Though summer kills the flowers, it leaves
  The leaves to fall in fall.
I would a story here commence,
  But you might find it stale ;
So let's suppose that we have reached
  The tail end of our tale."

SPELLING REFORM.

" With tragic air the love-lorn heir
  Once chased the chaste Louise ;
She quickly guessed her guest was there
  To please her with his pleas.

Now at her side he kneeling sighed,
  His sighs of woeful size ;
' Oh, hear me here, for lo, most low
  I rise before your eyes.

' This soul is sole thine own, Louise—
  'Twill never wean, I ween,
The love that I for aye shall feel,
  Though mean may be its mien ! '

'You know I cannot tell you no,'
　The maid made answer true ;
I love you aught, as sure I ought—
　To you 'tis due I do !'

'Since you are won, Oh fairest one,
　The marriage rite is right—
The chapel aisle I'll lead you up
　This night,' exclaimed the knight."
　　　　　　　— Yonkers' Gazette, U.S.

OWED TO MY CREDITORS.

" In vain I lament what is past,
　And pity their woe-begone looks,
Though they grin at the credit they gave,
　I know I am in their best books.
To my *tailor* my *breaches* of faith,
　On my conscience now but lightly sit,
For such lengths in his *measures* he's gone,
　He has given me many a *fit*.
My bootmaker, finding at *last*
　That my *soul* was too stubborn to suit,
Waxed wroth when he found he had got
　Anything but the *length of my foot*.
My hatmaker cunningly *felt*
　He'd seen many like me before,
So *brim*ful of insolence, vowed
　On credit he'd crown me no more.
My baker was *crusty* and *burnt*,
　When he found himself quite *overdone*

By a *fancy-bred* chap like myself,—
    Ay, as *cross* as a *Good Friday's bun.*
Next, my laundress, who washed pretty clean,
    In behaviour was dirty and bad ;
For into hot water she popped
    All the shirts and the dickies I had.
Then my butcher, who'd little at *stake,*
    Most surlily opened his *chops,*
And swore my affairs out of *joint,*
    So on to my carcase he pops.
In my lodgings exceedingly high,
    Though low in the rent to be sure,
Without warning my landlady seized,
    Took my things and the key of the door.
Thus cruelly used by the world,
    In the Bench I can smile at its hate ;
For a time I must alter my *style,*
    For I cannot get out of the *gate.*"

An Original Love Story.

" He struggled to kiss her.　She struggled the same
    To prevent him, so bold and undaunted ;
But, as smitten by lightning, he heard her exclaim,
    'Avaunt, sir !' and off he avaunted.

But when he returned, with the fiendishest laugh,
    Showing clearly that he was affronted,
And threatened by main force to carry her off,
    She cried ' Don't !' and the poor fellow donted.

When he meekly approached, and sat down at her feet,
　Praying aloud, as before he had ranted,
That she would forgive him and try to be sweet,
　And said, ' Can't you !' the dear girl recanted.

Then softly he whispered, ' How could you do so ?
　I certainly thought I was jilted ;
But come thou with me, to the parson we'll go ;
　Say, wilt thou, my dear ?' and she wilted."

PREVALENT POETRY.

" A wandering tribe, called the Siouxs,
　Wear moccasins, having no shiouxs.
　　　They are made of buckskin,
　　　With the fleshy side in,
　Embroidered with beads of bright hyiouxs.

When out on the war-path, the Siouxs
March single file—never by tiouxs—
　　　And by ' blazing ' the trees
　　　Can return at their ease,
And their way through the forests ne'er liouxs.

All new-fashioned boats he eschiouxs,
And uses the birch-bark caniouxs ;
　　　These are handy and light,
　　　And, inverted at night,
Give shelter from storms and from dyiouxs.

The principal food of the Siouxs
Is Indian maize, which they briouxs

And hominy make,
Or mix in a cake,
And eat it with fork, as they chiouxs."
—*Scribner's Magazine.*

A Temperance Sermon.

" If for a stomach ache you tache
Each time some whisky, it will break
You down and meak you sheak and quache,
And you will see a horrid snache.

Much whisky doth your wits beguile,
Your breath defuile, yourself make vuile ;
You lose your style, likewise your pyle,
If you erewhyle too often smuile.

But should there be, like now, a drought,
When water and your strength give ought,
None will your good name then malign
If you confign your drink to wign."
—*H. C. Dodge.*

" There was a young man in Bordeaux,
He said to himself—' Oh, heaux !
The girls have gone back on me seaux,
What to do I really don't kneaux.' "

TECHNICAL VERSE.

ANTICIPATORY DIRGE ON PROFESSOR BUCKLAND,
THE GEOLOGIST.

BY BISHOP SHUTTLEWORTH.

"MOURN, Ammonites, mourn o'er his funeral
    urn,
  Whose neck ye must grace no more;
Gneiss, Granite, and Slate !—he settled your date,
  And his ye must now deplore.
Weep, Caverns, weep ! with infiltering drip,
  Your recesses he'll cease to explore ;
For mineral veins or organic remains
  No Stratum again will he bore.

Oh ! his wit shone like crystal !—his knowledge pro-
    found
  From Gravel to Granite descended ;
No Trap could deceive him, no Slip could confound,
  Nor specimen, true or pretended.
He knew the birth-rock of each pebble so round,
  And how far its tour had extended.

His eloquence rolled like the Deluge retiring,
  Which Mastodon carcases floated ;

To a subject obscure he gave charms so inspiring
   Young and old on Geology doated.
He stood forth like an Outlier ; his hearers admiring
   In pencil each anecdote noted.

Where shall we our great professor inter,
   That in peace may rest his bones ?
If we hew him a rocky sepulchre,
   He'll rise up and break the stones,
And examine each Stratum that lies around,
For he's quite in his element underground.

If with mattock and spade his body we lay
   In the common Alluvial soil ;
He'll start up and snatch those tools away
   Of his own geological toil ;
In a Stratum so young the professor disdains
That embedded should be his Organic Remains.

Then, exposed to the drip of some case-hard'ning
     spring,
   His carcase let Stalactite cover ;
And to Oxford the petrified sage let us bring,
   When he is encrusted all over,
There, mid Mammoths and Crocodiles, high on a
     shelf,
Let him stand as a Monument raised to himself."

When Professor Buckland's grave was being dug
in Islip churchyard, in August 1856, the men came
unexpectedly upon the solid limestone rock, which

they were obliged to blast with gunpowder. The
coincidence of this fact with some of the verses
in the above anticipatory dirge is somewhat remarkable.

The following is by Jacob F. Henrici, and
appeared originally in *Scribner's Magazine* for
November 1879:

A MICROSCOPIC SERENADE.

"Oh come, my love, and seek with me
 A realm by grosser eye unseen,
Where fairy forms will welcome thee,
 And dainty creatures hail thee queen.
In silent pools the tube I'll ply,
 Where green conferva-threads lie curled,
And proudly bring to thy bright eye
 The trophies of the protist world.

We'll rouse the stentor from his lair,
 And gaze into the cyclops' eye ;
In chara and nitella hair
 The protoplasmic stream descry,
For ever weaving to and fro
 With faint molecular melody;
And curious rotifers I'll show,
 And graceful vorticellidæ.

Where melicertæ ply their craft
 We'll watch the playful water-bear,

And no envenomed hydra's shaft
Shall mar our peaceful pleasure there ;
But while we whisper love's sweet tale
We'll trace, with sympathetic art,
Within the embryonic snail
The growing rudimental heart.

Where rolls the volvox sphere of green,
And plastids move in Brownian dance—
If, wandering 'mid that gentle scene,
Two fond amœbæ shall perchance
Be changed to one beneath our sight
By process of biocrasis,
We'll recognise, with rare delight,
A type of our prospective bliss.

Oh dearer thou by far to me
In thy sweet maidenly estate
Than any seventy-fifth could be,
Of aperture however great !
Come, go with me, and we will stray
Through realm by grosser eye unseen,
Where protophytes shall homage pay,
And protozoa hail thee queen."

The epitaph following was written by the learned
and witty Dr. Charles Smith, author of the histories
of Cork and Waterford. It was read at a meeting
of the Dublin Medico-Philosophical Society on
July 1, 1756, and is a very curious specimen of the
"terminology of chemistry : "

"BOYLE GODFREY, CHYMIST AND DOCTOR OF MEDICINE.

EPITAPHIUM CHEMICUM.

Here lieth to digest, macerate, and amalgamate with clay,
In Balneo Arenæ,
Stratum super stratum,
The Residuum, Terra Damnata, and Caput Mortuum,
Of Boyle Godfrey, Chimist,
And M.D.
A man who in this earthly Laboratory
Pursued various processes to obtain
Arcanum Vitæ,
Or the secret to Live ;
Also Aurum Vitæ,
Or the art of getting, rather than making, Gold.
Alchemist like,
All his labour and propition,
As Mercury in the fire, evaporated in fumo.
When he dissolved to his first principles,
He departed as poor
As the last drops of an alembic ;
For riches are not poured
On the Adepts of this world.
Thus,
Not Solar in his purse,
Neither Lunar in his disposition,
Nor Jovial in his temperament ;
Being of Saturnine habit,
Venereal conflicts had left him,
And Martial ones he disliked.

With nothing saline in his composition,
All Salts but two were his Nostrums.
The Attic he did not know,
And that of the Earth he thought not Essential ;
But, perhaps, his had lost its savour.
Though fond of news, he carefully avoided
The fermentation, effervescence,
And decupilation of this life.
Full seventy years his exalted essence
Was hermetically sealed in its terrene matrass ;
But the radical moisture being exhausted,
The Elixir Vitæ spent,
Inspissated and exsiccated to a cuticle,
He could not suspend longer in his vehicle,
But precipitated gradatim
Per companum
To his original dust.
May that light, brighter than Bolognian Phosphorus,
Preserve him from the Incineration and Concremation
Of the Athanor, Empyreuma, and Reverberatory
Furnace of the other world,
Depurate him, like Tartarus Regeneratus,
From the Fœces and Scoria of this ;
Highly rectify and volatilize
His Etherial Spirit,
Bring it over the helm of the Retort of this Globe,
Place in a proper Recipient,
Or Crystalline Orb,
Among the elect of the Flowers of Benjamin,

Never to be saturated
Till the general Resuscitation,
Deflagration, and Calcination of all Things,
When all the reguline parts
Of his comminuted substance
Shall be again concentrated,
Revivified, alcoholized,
And imbibe its pristine Archeses ;
Undergo a new transmutation,
Eternal fixation,
And combination of its former Aura ;
Be coated over and decorated in robes more fair
Than the majestie of Bismuth,
More sparkling than Cinnabar,
Or Aurum Mosaicum.
And being found Proof Spirit,
Then to be exalted and sublimed together
Into the Concave Dome
Of the highest Aludel in Paradise."

To CLARA MORCHELLA DELICIOSA.

(A MYCOLOGICAL SERENADE.)

By Mr. A. Stephen Wilson, North Kinmundy, Aberdeenshire, and
read at a meeting of the Cryptogamic Society at Glasgow in 1880.

"Oh, lovely Clara, hie with me
    Where Cryptogams in beauty spore,
Corticiums creep on trunk and tree,
    And fairy rings their curves restore ;
Mycelia there pervade the ground,
    And many a painted pileus rear,

Agarics rend their veils around
   The ranal overture to hear.

Where gay Pezizæ flaunt their hues,
   A microscopic store we'll glean,
To sketch with camera the views
   In which the ascus may be seen.
Beneath our millemetric gaze
   Sporidia's length will stand revealed,
And eyes like thine will trace the maze
   In each hymenium concealed.

Æstivum tubers we shall dig,
   Like Suidæ in Fagian shade,
And many a Sphæria-sheltering twig
   Will in our vascula be laid.
For hard Sclerotia we shall peer,
   In barks and brassicaceous leaves,
And trace their progress through the year,
   Like Bobbies on the track of thieves.

While sages deem Solanum sent
   To succour Homo's hungry maw,
We'll prize it for development
   Of swelling Peronospora.
We'll mount the Myxogastre's threads
   To watch Plasmodium's vital flow,
While Capillitia lift their heads
   Generic mysteries to show.

I'll bring thee where the Chantarelles
   Inspire a mycologic theme,

Where Phallus in the shadow smells,
  And scarlet Amanita gleam ;
And lead thee where M'Moorlan's rye
  Is waving black with ergot spurs,
And many a Trichobasian dye
  Gives worth to corn and prickly burs.

And when the beetle calls us home,
  We'll gather on our lingering way
The violaceous Inolome
  And russet Alutacea,
The brown Boletus edulis
  Our fishing baskets soon will fill—
We'll dine on fungi fried in bliss,
  Nor dread the peck of butcher's bill."

To the Pliocene Skull.
(A geological address.)

"'Speak, O man, less recent !   Fragmentary fossil !
Primal pioneer of pliocene formation,
Hid in lowest drifts below the earliest stratum
      Of volcanic tufa !

'Older than the beasts, the oldest Palæotherium ;
Older than the trees, the oldest Cryptogami ;
Older than the hills, those infantile eruptions
      Of earth's epidermis !

'Eo—Mio— Plio—whatso'er the "cene" was
That those vacant sockets filled with awe and wonder,—
Whether shores Devonian or Silurian beaches,—
      Tell us thy strange story !

'Or has the professor slightly antedated
By some thousand years thy advent on this planet,
Giving thee an air that's somewhat better fitted
     For cold-blooded creatures?

'Wert thou true spectator of that mighty forest
When above thy head the stately Sigillaria
Reared its columned trunks in that remote and distant
     Carboniferous epoch?

'Tell us of that scene,—the dim and watery woodland,
Songless, silent, hushed, with never bird or insect,
Veiled with spreading fronds and screened with tall
   club-mosses,
     Lycopodiacea,—

'When beside thee walked the solemn Plesiosaurus,
And around thee crept the festive Ichthyosaurus,
While from time to time above thee flew and circled
     Cheerful Pterodactyls.

'Tell us of thy food,—those half-marine refections,
Crinoids on the shell and Brachiopods *au naturel,*—
Cuttlefish to which the *pieuvre* of Victor Hugo
     Seems a periwinkle.

'Speak, thou awful vestige of the earth's creation,—
Solitary fragment of remains organic !
Tell the wondrous secret of thy past existence,—
     Speak ! thou oldest primate !'

Even as I gazed, a thrill of the maxilla,
And a lateral movement of the condyloid process,

With post-pliocene sounds of healthy mastication,
 Ground the teeth together.

And, from that imperfect dental exhibition,
Stained with express juices of the weed Nicotian,
Came these hollow accents, blent with softer murmurs
 Of expectoration :

' Which my name is Bowers, and my crust was busted
Falling down a shaft in Calaveras County,
But I'd take it kindly if you'd send the pieces
 Home to old Missouri ! ' "
        —Bret Harte.

The following verses are from "Notes and Queries," and evidently refer to a case of "breach of promise":

KNOX WARD, KING-AT-ARMS, DISARMED AT LAW.

" Ye fair injured nymphs, and ye beaus who deceive 'em,
Who with passion engage, and without reason leave 'em,
Draw near and attend how the Hero I sing
Was foiled by a Girl, though at Arms he was King.

Crest, mottoes, supporters, and *bearings* knew he,
And deeply was studied in old pedigree.
He would sit a whole evening, and, not without rapture,
Tell who begat who to the end of the Chapter.

In forming his *tables* nought grieved him so sorely
That the man died *Cœlebs,* or else *sine prole.*
At last, having traced other families down,
He began to have thoughts of increasing his own.

A Damsel he chose, not too slow of belief,
And fain would be deemed her admirer *in chief.*

He *blazoned* his suit, and the sum of his tale
Was his *field* and her *field* joined *party per pale.*

In different style, to tie faster the noose,
He next would attack her in soft *billet doux.*
His *argent* and *sable* were laid aside quite,
Plain *English* he wrote, and in plain black and white.

Against such *atchievements* what beauty could fence?
Or who would have thought it was all but *pretence?*—
His pain to relieve, and fulfil his desire,
The lady agreed to join hands with the squire.

The squire, in a fret that the jest went so far,
Considered with speed how to put in a *bar.*
His words bound not him, since hers did not confine her:
And that is plain law, because Miss is a *minor.*

Miss briskly replied that the law was too hard,
If she, who's a *minor*, may not be a *ward.*
In law then confiding, she took it upon her,
By justice to mend those foul breaches of honour.

She handled him so that few would, I warrant,
Have been in his *coat* on so *sleeveless* an errant.
She made him give bond for stamped *argent* and *or*,
And *sabled* his shield with *gules* blazoned before.

Ye heralds produce, from the time of the Normans,
In all your Records such a *base* non-performance;
Or if without instance the case is we touch on,
Let this be set down as a *blot* in his *scutcheon.*"

LAMENT OF AN UNFORTUNATE DRUGGIST,

A Member of the Pharmaceutical Society, whose matrimonial
speculations have been disappointed.

" You that have charge of wedded love, take heed
  To keep the vessel which contains it air-tight;

So that no oxygen may enter there !
Lest (like as in a keg of elder wine,
The which, when made, thy careless hand forgot
To bung securely down) full soon, alas !
Acetous fermentation supervene
And winter find thee wineless, and, instead
Of wine, afford thee nought but vinegar.

    Thus hath it been with me : there was a time
When neither rosemary nor jessamine,
Cloves or verbena, maréchale, resedé,
Or e'en great Otto's self, were more delicious
Unto my nose, than Betsy to mine eyes ;
And, in our days of courtship, I have thought
That my career through life, with her, would be
Bright as my own show-bottles ; but, ah me !
It was a vision'd scene.   From what she *was*
To what she *is*, is as the pearliness
Of Creta Præp. compared with Antim. Nig.
There was a time she was all Almond-mixture
(A bland emulsion ; I can recommend it
To him who hath a cold), but now, woe ! woe !
She is a fierce and foaming combination
Of turpentine with vitriolic oil.

    Oh ! name not Sulphur, when you speak of her,
For she is Brimstone's very incarnation,
She is the Bitter-apple of my life,
The Scillæ oxymel of my existence,
That knows no sweets with her.

    What shall I do ?—where fly ?—What Hellebore

Can ease the madness that distracts my brain !
What aromatic vinegar restore
The drooping memory of brighter days !
They bid me seek relief in Prussic acid ;
They tell me Arsenic holds a mighty power
To put to flight each ill and care of life :
They mention Opium, too ; they say its essence,
Called Battley's Sedative, can steep the soul
Chin-deep in blest imaginings ; till grief
Changed by its chemic agency, becomes
One lump of blessed Saccharum ;--these things
They tell to *me—me*, who for twelve long years
Have triturated drugs for a subsistence,
From seven i' th' morn until the midnight hour.
I have no faith in physic's agency
E'en when most ' genuine,' for I have seen
And analysed its nature, and I know
That Humbug is its Active Principle,
Its ultimate and Elemental Basis.
What then is left ?   No more to Fate I'll bend :
I will rush into chops ! and Stout shall be—my end ! ! "

—*Punch* (1844.)

ODE TO " DAVIES' ANALYTICAL."

" Charming chaos, glorious puddle,
Ethics opaque, book of bliss ;
Through thy platitudes I waddle,
O thou subtle synthesis !

To thy soft consideration,
　Give I talents, give I time ;
Though ' perpetual occultation '
　Shuts me from thy balmy clime.

As unto the sea-tossed trader,
　Is the guiding Polar Star ;
Thou'rt my ' zenith ' and my 'nadir,'
　Still ' so near and yet so far.'

Sancho never loved his gravies
　As I love thy sunny face ;
Sheep-bound master-piece of Davies,
　Benefactor of his race !

Man nor god, not even 'ox-eyed
　Juno,' could me from thee part ;
My 'enthymeme,' my sweet 'protoxide,'
　Thou'rt the 'zeugma' of my heart.

When were built the rocks azoic,
　Sat'st thou on the granite hill ;
And with constancy heroic,
　To *me* thou art azoic still.

My 'syzygy,' I'll ne'er leave thee,
　Thou shalt ne'er from me escheat ;
I will cherish thee, believe me,
　Pythagorean obsolete.

Bless me in the midnight watches,
　Ever by my pillow keep
Ruler, chalk, and black-board scratches,
　Lovely nightmare, while I sleep.

Be 'co-ordinate' for ever,
   For ever my 'abscissa' be ;
The Fates can overwhelm me n ever,
   Whilst *thou* art in 'perigee.'"

MAN AND THE ASCIDIAN.

A MORALITY IN THE QUEEN ANNE MANNER.

"The Ancestor remote of Man,
Says D—w—n, is th' Ascidian,
A scanty sort of water-beast
That, 90,000,000 years at least
Before Gorillas came to be,
Went swimming up and down the sea.

Their ancestors the pious praise,
And like to imitate their ways ;
How, then, does our first parent live,
What lesson has his life to give ?

Th' Ascidian tadpole, young and gay,
Doth Life with one bright eye survey,
His consciousness has easy play.
He's sensitive to grief and pain,
Has tail, and spine, and bears a brain,
And everything that fits the state
Of creatures we call vertebrate.
But age comes on ; with sudden shock
He sticks his head against a rock !
His tail drops off, his eye drops in,
His brain's absorbed into his skin ;

L

He does not move, nor feel, nor know
The tidal water's ebb and flow,
But still abides, unstirred, alone,
A sucker sticking to a stone.
And we, his children, truly we
In youth are, like the Tadpole, free.
And where we would we blithely go,
Have brain and hearts, and feel and know.
Then Age comes on!   To Habit we
Affix ourselves and are not free ;
Th' Ascidian's rooted to a rock,
And we are bond-slaves of the clock ;
Our rock is Medicine—Letters—Law,
From these our heads we cannot draw :
Our loves drop off, our hearts drop in,
And daily thicker grows our skin.
We scarcely live, we scarcely know
The wide world's moving ebb and flow,
The clanging currents ring and shock,
But we are rooted to the rock.
And thus at ending of his span,
Blind, deaf, and indolent, does Man
Revert to the Ascidian."

    —*St. James's Gazette* (*July* 1880).

A Geological Madrigal.

" I have found out a gift for my fair ;
 I know where the fossils abound,
Where the footprints of *Aves* declare
 The birds that once walked on the ground ;

Oh, come, and—in technical speech—
  We'll walk this Devonian shore,
Or on some Silurian beach
  We'll wander, my love, evermore.

I will show thee the sinuous track
  By the slow-moving Annelid made,
Or the Trilobite that, farther back,
  In the old Potsdam sandstone was laid ;
Thou shalt see in his Jurassic tomb,
  The Plesiosaurus embalmed ;
In his Oolitic prime and his bloom
  Iguanodon safe and unharmed !

You wished—I remember it well,
  And I loved you the more for that wish—
For a perfect cystedian shell
  And a *whole* holocephalic fish.
And oh, if Earth's strata contains
  In its lowest Silurian drift,
Or palæozoic remains
  The same—'tis your lover's free gift.

Then come, love, and never say nay,
  But calm all your maidenly fears ;
We'll note, love, in one summer's day
  The record of millions of years ;
And though the Darwinian plan
  Your sensitive feelings may shock,   ·
We'll find the beginning of man—
  Our fossil ancestors, in rock !"

                          —*Bret Harte.*

THE HUSBAND'S COMPLAINT.

"Will she thy linen wash and hosen darn?"—GAY.

" I'm utterly sick of this hateful alliance
Which the ladies have formed with impractical Science !
They put out their washing to learn hydrostatics,
And give themselves airs for the sake of pneumatics.

They are knowing in muriate, and nitrate, and chlorine,
While the stains gather fast on the walls and the flooring—
And the jellies and pickles fall woefully short,
With their chemical use of the still and retort.

Our expenses increase (without drinking French wines),
For they keep no accounts, with their tangents and sines—
And to make both ends meet they give little assistance,
With their accurate sense of the squares of the distance.

They can name every spot from Peru to El Arish,
Except just the bounds of their own native parish ;
And they study the orbits of Venus and Saturn,
While their home is resigned to the thief and the slattern.

Chronology keeps back the dinner two hours,
The smoke-jack stands still while they learn motive powers;
Flies and shells swallow up all our everyday gains,
And our acres are mortgaged for fossil remains.

They cease to reflect with their talk of refraction—
They drive us from home by electric attraction—
And I'm sure, since they've bothered their heads with
　　affinity
I'm repulsed every hour from my learned divinity.

When the poor stupid husband is weary and starving,
Anatomy leads them to give up the carving ;
And we drudges the shoulder of mutton must buy,
While they study the line of the *os humeri.*

If we 'scape from our troubles to take a short nap,
We awake with a din about limestone and trap ;

And the fire is extinguished past regeneration,
For the women were wrapt in the deep-coal formation.

'Tis an impious thing that the wives of the laymen
Should use Pagan words 'bout a pistil and stamen ;
Let the heir break his head while they foster a Dahlia,
And the babe die of pap as they talk of mammalia.

The first son becomes half a fool in reality,
While the mother is watching his large ideality ;
And the girl roars unchecked, quite a moral abortion,
For we trust her benevolence, order, and caution.

I sigh for the good times of sewing and spinning,
Ere this new tree of knowledge had set them a sinning ;
The women are mad, and they'll build female colleges,—
So here's to plain English !—a plague on their 'ologies !"

HOMŒOPATHIC SOUP.

"Take a robin's leg
(Mind ! the drumstick merely),
  Put it in a tub
Filled with water nearly ;
  Set it out of doors,
In a place that's shady,
  Let it stand a week
(Three days if for a lady).

  Drop a spoonful of it
In a five-pail kettle,
  Which may be made of tin
Or any baser metal ;
  Fill the kettle up,
Set it on a boiling,
  Strain the liquor well,
To prevent its oiling ;

  One atom add of salt,
For the thickening one rice
    kernel,

And use to light the fire
The Homœopathic Journal.
  Let the liquor boil
Half an hour or longer
  (If 'tis for a man,
Of course you'll make it
    stronger).

  Should you now desire
That the soup be flavoury,
  Stir it once around
With a stalk of Savory.
  When the broth is made,
Nothing can excel it :
  Then three times a day
Let the patient *smell* it.
  If he chance to die,
Say 'twas Nature did it ;
  If he chance to live,
Give the soup the credit."

A BILLET-DOUX.

BY A COUNTRY SCHOOLMASTER, CHIDDINGLY, SUSSEX.

" Accept, dear Miss, this *article* of mine,
(For what's *indefinite*, who can *define ?*)
My *case* is singular, my house is rural,
Wilt thou, indeed, consent to make it *plural ?*
Something, I feel, pervades my system through,
I can't describe, yet *substantively* true.
Thy form so *feminine*, thy mind reflective,
Where all's *possessive* good, and nought *objective*,
I'm *positive* none can *compare* with thee
In wit and worth's *superlative* degree.
First person, then, *indicative* but prove,
Let thy soft *passive* voice exclaim, ' I LOVE !'
Active, in cheerful *mood*, no longer *neuter*,
I'll leave my cares, both *present, past*, and *future.*
But ah! what torture must I undergo
Till I obtain that little ' Yes ' or ' No !'
Spare me the *negative*—to save compunction,
Oh, let my *preposition* meet *conjunction.*
What could excite such pleasing recollection,
At hearing thee pronounce this *interjection*,
' I will be thine ! thy joys and griefs to share,
Till Heaven shall please to *point* a *period* there'!"
                                    —*Family Friend* (1849).

Cumulative verse—in which one newspaper gives
a few lines, and other papers follow it up—like that
which follows, is very common in American newspapers, which, however profound or dense, invari-
ably have a corner for this kind of thing. It has
been said that the reason why no purely comic

paper, like *Punch* or *Fun*, succeeds in the United States, is because all their papers have a "funny" department.

THE ARAB AND HIS DONKEY.

An Arab came to the river side,
　With a donkey bearing an obelisk ;
But he would not try to ford the tide,
　For he had too good an ＊.
　　　　　　　　　　　—Boston Globe.

So he camped all night by the river side,
　And remained till the tide had ceased to swell,
For he knew should the donkey from life subside,
　He never would find its ‖.
　　　　　　　　　　　—Salem Sunbeam.

When the morning dawned, and the tide was out,
　The pair crossed over 'neath Allah's protection ;
And the Arab was happy, we have no doubt,
　For he had the best donkey in all that §.
　　　　　　　　　　　—Somerville Journal.

You are wrong, they were drowned in crossing over,
　Though the donkey was bravest of all his race ;
He luxuriates now in horse-heaven clover,
　And his master has gone to the Prophet's *em*⁓
　　　　　　　　　　—Elevated Railway Journal.

These assinine poets deserved to be "blowed,"
　Their rhymes being faulty, and frothy and beery ;

What really befell the ass and its load
Will ever remain a desolate ?.

    —*Paper and Print.*

Our Yankee friends, with all their ——
For once, we guess, their mark have missed ;
And with poetry *Paper and Print* is rash
In damming its flow with its editor's ☞

In parable and moral leave a **:** between,   [*Space*]
For reflection, or your wits fall out of joint ;
The "Arab," ye see, is a printing machine,
And the donkey is he who can't see the •

    —*British and Colonial Printer.*

An Ohio poet thus sings of the beginning of
man :

EVOLUTION.

   " O sing a song of phosphates,
       Fibrine in a line,
   Four and twenty follicles
       In the van of time.

   When the phosphorescence
       Evoluted brain,
   Superstition ended,
       Man began to reign."

SINGLE-RHYMED VERSE.

HE following lines are from a book written by M. Halpine, under the sobriquet of "Private Miles O'Reilly," during the Civil War in the United States. They have some merit apart from their peculiar versification, and the idea of comparing the "march past" of veteran troops in war time with the parade of the old gladiators is a happy one.

MORITURI TE SALUTANT.

"'*Morituri te salutant!*' say the soldiers as they pass;
  Not in uttered words they say it, but we feel it as they pass—
  'We, who are about to perish, we salute thee as we pass!'
  Nought of golden pomp and glitter mark the veterans as they
    pass—
  Travel-stained, but bronzed and sinewy, firmly, proudly, how they
    pass;
  And we hear them, '*Morituri te salutant!*' as they pass.
  On his pawing steed, the General marks the waves of men that
    pass,
  And his eyes at times are misty, now are blazing, as they pass,
  For his breast with pride is swelling, as the stalwart veterans pass,
  Gallant chiefs their swords presenting, trail them proudly as they
    pass—

Battle banners, torn and glorious, dip saluting as they pass ;
Brazen clangours shake the welkin, as the manly squadrons pass.
Oh, our comrades ! gone before us, in the last review to pass,
Never more to earthly chieftain dipping colours as you pass,
Heaven accord you gentle judgment when before the Throne you
    pass ! ''

"About the year 1775 there was a performer named Cervetti in the orchestra of Drury Lane Theatre, to whom the gods had given the appropriate name of Nosey, from his enormous staysail, that helped to carry him before the wind. 'Nosey !' shouted from the galleries, was the signal, or word of command, for the fiddlers to strike up. This man was originally an Italian merchant of good repute; but failing in business, he came over to England, and adopted music for a profession. He had a notable knack of loud yawning, with which he sometimes unluckily filled up Garrick's expressive pauses, to the infinite annoyance of Garrick and the laughter of the audience. In the summer of 1777 he played at Vauxhall, at the age of ninety-eight." Upon such another nose was the following lines written:

THE ROMAN NOSE.

"That Roman nose ! that Roman nose !
  Has robbed my bosom of repose ;
  For when in sleep my eyelids close,
  It haunts me still, that Roman nose !

Between two eyes as black as sloes
The bright and flaming ruby glows :
That Roman nose ! that Roman nose !
And beats the blush of damask rose.

I walk the streets, the alleys, rows ;
I look at all the Jems and Joes ;
And old and young, and friends and foes,
But cannot find a Roman nose !

Then blessed be the day I chose
That nasal beauty of my beau's ;
And when at last to Heaven I goes,
I hope to spy his Roman nose !"

—Merrie England.

Mrs. Thrale, on her thirty-fifth birthday, remarked to Dr. Johnson, that no one would send
her verses now that she had attained that age,
upon which the Doctor, without the least hesita-
tion, recited the following lines :

THIRTY-FIVE.

"Oft in danger, yet alive,
  We are come to thirty-five ;
  Long may better years arrive,
  Better years than thirty-five.
  Could philosophers contrive
  Life to stop at thirty-five,
  Time his hours should never drive
  O'er the bounds of thirty-five.

High to soar, and deep to dive,
Nature gives at thirty-five ;
Ladies, stock and tend your hive,
Trifle not at thirty-five ;
For, howe'er we boast and strive,
Life declines from thirty-five ;
He that ever hopes to thrive,
Must begin by thirty-five ;
And all who wisely wish to wive,
Must look on Thrale at thirty-five."

Moore, in his "Life of Sheridan," says that he
(Sheridan) "had a sort of hereditary fancy for
difficult trifling in poetry ; particularly to that sort
which consists in rhyming to the same word through
a long string of couplets, till every rhyme that the
language supplies for it is exhausted," a task which
must have required great patience and persever-
ance. Moore quotes some dozen lines entitled
"To Anne," wherein a lady is made to bewail the
loss of her trunk, and she thus rhymes her lamen-
tations :

" Have you heard, my dear Anne, how my spirits are sunk ?
Have you heard of the cause ?   Oh, the loss of my trunk !
From exertion or firmness I've never yet slunk,
But my fortitude's gone with the loss of my trunk !
Stout Lucy, my maid, is a damsel of spunk,
Yet she weeps night and day for the loss of my trunk !

I'd better turn nun, and coquet with a monk,
For with whom can I flirt without aid from my trunk ?

. . . .

Accursed be the thief, the old rascally hunks,
Who rifles the fair, and lays hold on their trunks !
He who robs the king's stores of the least bit of junk,
Is hanged—while he's safe who has plundered my trunk !
There's a phrase among lawyers when *nunc*'s put for *tunc;*
But *nunc* and *tunc* both, must I grieve for my trunk !
Huge leaves of that great commentator, old Brunck,
Perhaps was the paper that lined my poor trunk!" &c. &c.

From another of these trifles of Sheridan, Moore
gives the following extracts :

" Muse, assist me to complain,
While I grieve for Lady Jane ;
I ne'er was in so sad a vein,
Deserted now by Lady Jane.

Lord Petre's house was built by Payne,
No mortal architect made Jane.
If hearts had windows, through the pane
Of mine, you'd see Lady Jane.

At breakfast I could scarce refrain
From tears at missing Lady Jane ;
Nine rolls I ate, in hope to gain
The roll that might have fallen to Jane."

John Skelton, a poet of the fifteenth century, in
great repute as a wit and satirist, was inordinately
fond of writing in lines of three or four syllables,

and also of iteration of rhyme. This perhaps was
the cause of his writing much that was mere doggerel, as this style scarcely admits of the convey-
ance of serious sentiment. Occasionally, however,
his miniature lines are interesting, as in this address
to Mrs. Margaret Hussey:

"Merry Margaret,
　As midsummer flower,
　Gentle as falcon,
　Or hawk of the tower,
　With solace and gladness,
　Much mirth and no madness,
　All good and no badness,
　So joyously,
　So maidenly,
　So womanly,

Her demeaning,
In everything
Far, far passing
That I can indite
Or suffice to write
Of merry Margaret,
As midsummer flower,
Gentle as falcon,
Or hawk of the tower."

The following national pasquinade we find in
Egerton Brydges' "Censura Literaria Restituta,"
written in commemoration of the failure of Spain
by her Invincible Armada to invade Britain. The
iteration of metre is all that approaches in it to
the style of Skelton, of whose verse it is an imitation:

"A Skeltonical salutation
　Or condign gratulation,
　At the just vexation
　Of the Spanish nation,
　That in a bravado
　Spent many a crusado
　In setting forth an Armado
　England to invado.
　Pro cujus memoria

Ye may well be soria,
Full small may be your gloria
When ye shall hear this storia,
Then will ye cry and roria,
We shall see her no moria.
O king of Spaine!
Is it not a paine
To thy hearte and braine,
And every vaine,

To see thy traine
For to sustaine
Withouten gaine,
The world's disdaine ;
Which despise
As toies and lies,
With shoutes and cries,
Thy enterprise ;
As fitter for pies
And butterflies
Then men so wise ?
O waspish king !
Where's now thy sting.
The darts or sling,
Or strong bowstring,
That should us wring,
And under bring ?
Who every way

Thee vexe and pay
And beare the sway
By night and day,
To thy dismay
In battle array,
And every fray ?
O pufte with pride !
What foolish guide
Made thee provide
To over-ride
This land so wide,
From side to side ;
And then untride,
Away to slide,
And not to abide ;
But all in a ring
Away to fling ?"
&c.　&c.

EPITAPH ON DR. WILLIAM MAGINN.

" Here, early to bed, lies kind William Maginn,
Who with genius, wit, learning, life's trophies to win,
Had neither great lord, nor rich cit of his kin,
Nor discretion to set himself up as to tin ;
So his portion soon spent, like the poor heir of Lynn,
He turned author, ere yet there was beard on his chin ;
And whoever was out, or whoever was in,
For your Tories his fine Irish brains he would spin ;
Who received prose and verse with a promising grin,
' Go a-head, you queer fish, and more power to your fin ! '
But to save from starvation stirr'd never a pin.
Light for long was his heart, tho' his breeches were thin,
Else his acting, for certain, was equal to Quin :
But at last he was beat, and sought help of the bin :

(All the same to the doctor, from claret to gin !)
Which led swiftly to gaol, with consumption therein.
It was much, when the bones rattled loose in the skin,
He got leave to die here, out of Babylon's din.*
Barring drink and the girls, I ne'er heard of a sin,—
Many worse, better few, than bright, broken Maginn ! "

THE MUSICAL ASS.

" The fable which I now present,
Occurred to me by accident:
And whether bad or excellent,
Is merely so by accident.

A stupid ass this morning went
Into a field by accident:
And cropped his food, and was content,
Until he spied by accident
A flute, which some oblivious gent
Had left behind by accident;
When, sniffing it with eager scent,
He breathed on it by accident,
And made the hollow instrument
Emit a sound by accident.
' Hurrah, hurrah ! ' exclaimed the brute,
' How cleverly I play the flute ! '

A fool, in spite of nature's bent,
May shine for once,—by accident."

* Maginn died at Walton-on-Thames, 21st August 1842. He was
one of the gayest, brightest, and wittiest of those reckless littera-
teurs who half a century ago worshipped with equal devotion at the
shrines of Apollo and Bacchus.

The above is a translation from the "Fabulas
Litterarias" of Tomaso de Yriarte (1750–1790).
Yriarte conceived the idea of making moral truths
the themes for fables in the style of Æsop, and
these he composed in every variety of verse which
seemed at all suitable. Even when the leading
idea presents no remarkable incident, Yriarte's
fables please by their simplicity.

BOXIANA.

"I hate the very name of box;
    It fills me full of fears;
It minds me of the woes I've felt
    Since I was young in years.

They sent me to a Yorkshire school,
    Where I had many knocks;
For there my schoolmates box'd my ears,
    Because I could not box.

I packed my box; I picked the locks,
    And ran away to sea;
And very soon I learnt to box
    The compass merrily.

I came ashore; I called a coach
    And mounted on the box:
The coach upset against a post,
    And gave me dreadful knocks.

I soon got well; in love I fell,
    And married Martha Box;

To please her will, at famed Box Hill
    I took a country box.

I had a pretty garden there,
    All bordered round with box ;
But ah ! alas ! there lived next door
    A certain Captain Knox.

He took my wife to see the play ;—
    They had a private box :
I jealous grew, and from that day
    I hated Captain Knox.

I sold my house ; I left my wife ;
    And went to Lawyer Fox,
Who tempted me to seek redress
    All from a jury-box.

I went to law, whose greedy maw
    Soon emptied my strong box ;
I lost my suit, and cash to boot,
    All through that crafty Fox.

The name of box I therefore dread,
    I've had so many shocks ;
They'll never end ; for when I'm dead
    They'll nail me in a box."

THE RULING POWER.

" Gold ! Gold ! Gold ! Gold !
    Bright and yellow, hard and cold,
    Molten, graven, hammered, and rolled ;
    Heavy to get, and light to hold ;

Hoarded, bartered, bought and sold,
Stolen, borrowed, squandered, doled ;
Spurned by the young, but hugged by the old,
To the very verge of the churchyard mould ;
Price of many a crime untold ;
Gold ! Gold ! Gold ! Gold !
Good or bad, a thousandfold !"

—T. Hood.

NAHUM FAY ON THE LOSS OF HIS WIFE.

" Just eighteen years ago this day,
  Attired in all her best array—
  For she was airy, young, and gay,
  And loved to make a grand display,
  While I the charges would defray—
  My *Cara Sposa* went astray ;
  By night eloping in a sleigh,
  With one whose name begins with J,
  Resolved with me she would not stay,
  And be subjected to my sway ;
  Because I wish'd her to obey,
  Without reluctance or delay,
  And never interpose her nay,
  Nor any secrets e'er betray.
  But wives will sometimes have their way,
  And cause, if possible, a fray ;
  Then who so obstinate as they ?
  She therefore left my house for aye,
  Before my hairs had turned to gray,
  Or I'd sustained the least decay,

Which caused at first some slight dismay :
For I considered it foul play.
Now where she's gone I cannot say,
For I've not seen her since the day
When Johnston took her in his sleigh,
To his seductive arts a prey,
And posted off to Canada.
Now when her conduct I survey,
And in the scale of justice weigh,
Who blames me, if I do inveigh
Against her to my dying day?
But live as long as live I may,
I've always purposed not to pay
(Contract whatever debts she may)
A shilling for her ; but I pray
That when her body turns to clay,
If mourning friends should her convey
To yonder graveyard, they'll not lay
Her body near to Nahum Fay."

THE RADENOVITCH.

A SONG OF A NEW DANCE.

" Are you anxious to bewitch ?
You must learn the Radenovitch !
Would you gain of fame a niche ?
You must dance the Radenovitch !
'Mong the noble and the rich,
All the go's the Radenovitch !
It has got to such a pitch,
All must dance the Radenovitch !

If without a flaw or hitch
You can dance the Radenovitch,
Though you've risen from the ditch
(Yet have learned the Radenovitch),
You'll get on without a hitch,
Dancing of the Radenovitch.
If for glory you've an itch,
Learn to dance the Radenovitch;
And, though corns may burn and twitch,
While you foot the Radenovitch;
In your side though you've a stitch,
All along o' the Radenovitch,
You will gain an eminence which
You will owe the Radenovitch!
Therefore let the Maitre's switch
Teach your toes the Radenovitch!"

FOOTMAN JOE.

" Would you see a man that's slow?
Come and see our footman Joe:
Most unlike the bounding roe,
Or an arrow from a bow,
Or the flight direct of crow,
Is the pace of footman Joe;
Crabs that hobble to and fro,
In their motions copy Joe.
Snails, contemptuous as they go,
Look behind and laugh at Joe.
An acre any man may mow,
Ere across it crawleth Joe.

Trip on light fantastic toe,
Ye that tripping like, for Joe ;
Measured steps of solemn woe
Better suit with solid Joe.
Danube, Severn, Trent, and Po,
Backward to their source will flow
Ere despatch be made by Joe.
Letters to a Plenipo
Send not by our footman Joe.
Would you Job's full merit know,
Ring the bell, and wait for Joe ;
Whether it be king or no,
'Tis just alike to lazy Joe.
Legal process none can show,
If your lawyer move like Joe.
Death, at last, our common foe,
Must trip up the heels of Joe ;
And a stone shall tell—' Below,
Hardly changed, still sleepeth Joe.
Loud shall the final trumpet blow,
But the last comer will be Joe !' "

— *G. Hebert.*

To a Lady

WHO ASKED FOR A POEM OF NINETY LINES.

" Task a horse beyond his strength
And the horse will fail at length ;
Whip a dog, the poor dog whines—
Yet you ask for ninety lines.

Though you give me ninety quills,
Built me ninety paper-mills,
Showed me ninety inky Rhines,
I could not write ninety lines.

Ninety miles I'd walk for you,
Till my feet were black and blue;
Climb high hills, and dig deep mines,
But I can't write ninety lines.

Though my thoughts were thick as showers,
Plentiful as summer flowers,
Clustering like Italian vines,
I could not write ninety lines.

When you have drunk up the sea,
Floated ships in cups of tea,
Plucked the sun from where it shines,
Then I'll write you ninety lines.

Even the bard who lives on rhyme,
Teaching silly words to chime,
Seldom sleeps, and never dines,—
He could scarce write ninety lines.

Well you know my love is such,
You could never ask too much;
Yet even love itself declines
Such a work as ninety lines.

Though you frowned with ninety frowns,
Bribed me with twice ninety towns,

Offered me the starry signs,
I could not write ninety lines.

Many a deed I've boldly done
Since my race of life begun ;
But my spirit peaks and pines
When it thinks of ninety lines.

Long I hope for thee and me
Will our lease of this world be ;
But though hope our fate entwines,
Death will come ere ninety lines.

Ninety songs the birds will sing,
Ninety beads the child will string ;
But his life the poet tines,
If he aims at ninety lines.

Ask me for a thousand pounds,
Ask me for my house and grounds ;
Levy all my wealth in fines,
But don't ask for ninety lines.

I have ate of every dish—
Flesh of beast, and bird, and fish ;
Briskets, fillets, knuckles, chines,
But eating won't make ninety lines.

I have drunk of every cup,
Till I drank whole vineyards up ;
German, French, and Spanish wines,
But drinking won't make ninety lines.

Since, then, you have used me so,
To the Holy Land I'll go ;
And at all the holy shrines
I shall pray for ninety lines.

Ninety times a long farewell,
All my love I could not tell,
Though 'twas multiplied by nines,
Ninety times these ninety lines."
                                        —*H. G. Bell.*

We give the following curious old ballad a place
here, not only on account of the iteration of rhyme,
but also as the original of the macaronic verses
on p. 95 :

THE WIG AND THE HAT.

" The elderly gentleman's here,
    With his cane, his wig, and his hat ;
A good-humoured man all declare,
    But then he's o'erloaded with fat.

By the side of a murmuring stream
    This elderly gentleman sat ;
On the top of his head was his wig,
    And a-top of his wig was his hat.

The wind it blew high and blew strong,
    As this elderly gentleman sat,
And bore from his head in a trice
    And plunged in the river his hat.

The gentleman then took his cane,
  Which lay on his lap as he sat,
And dropped in the river his wig
  In attempting to get out his hat.

Cool reflection at length came across,
  While this elderly gentleman sat ;
So he thought he would follow the stream,
  And look for his fine wig and hat.

His breast it grew cold with despair,
  And full in his eye madness sat ;
So he flung in the river his cane,
  To swim with his wig and his hat.

His head, being thicker than common,
  O'er-balanced the rest of his fat,
And in plunged this son of a woman
  To follow his wig, cane, and hat.

A Newfoundland dog was at hand—
  No circumstance could be more pat—
The old man he brought safe to land,
  Then fetched out his wig, cane, and hat.

The gentleman, dripping and cold,
  Seem'd much like a half-drowned rat,
But praised his deliverer so bold,
  Then adjusted his cane, wig, and hat.

Now homeward the gentleman hied,
  But neither could wear wig or hat ;

The dog followed close at his side,
  Fawn'd, waggled his tail, and all that.

The gentleman, filled with delight,
  The dog's master hastily sought;
Two guineas set all things to right,
  For that sum his true friend he bought.

From him the dog never would part,
  But lived much caressed for some years;
Till levelled by Death's fatal dart,
  When the gentleman shed many tears.

Then buried poor Tray in the Green.
  And placed o'er the grave a small stone,
Whereon a few lines may be seen,
  Expressive of what he had done."

ANAGRAMS.

NAGRAMS are curious and frequently clever examples of formal literary trifling. Camden, in his "Remains," gave to the world a treatise showing that in his day anagrams were endowed with an undue and superstitious importance, being regarded as nothing less than the occult and mysterious finger of Fate, revealed in the names of men.

"The only quintessence," says this old writer, "that hitherto the alchemy of wit could draw out of names, is *anagrammatisme* or *metagrammatisme*, which is the dissolution of a name, truly written, into the letters as its elements, and a new connection of it by artificial transposition, without addition, subtraction, or change of any letter, into different words, making some perfect sense applicable to the person named." Precise anagrammatists adhere strictly to these rules, with the exception of omitting or retaining the letter *h* according to their convenience, alleging that *h* cannot claim the rights of a letter; others, again, think it no injury sometimes to use *e* for *æ*, *v* for *w*, *s* for *z*, *c* for *k*, and contrariwise, and several of the instances which follow will be found variously imperfect. Camden calls the charming difficulty of making an anagram, "the whetstone of patience to them that shall practise it ; for some have been seen to bite their pen, scratch their head, bend their brows, bite their lips, beat the board, tear their paper, when the names were fair for somewhat, and caught nothing therein,—yet, notwithstanding the sour sort of critics, good anagrams yield a delightful comfort and pleasant motion to honest minds."

Camden places the origin of the anagram as far back as the time of Moses, and conjectures that it may have had some share in the mystical traditions, afterwards called the "Cabala," communicated by the Jewish lawgiver. One part of the art of the cabalists lay in what they called *themuru* —that is, changing—or finding the hidden and mystical meaning in names, which they did by transposing and fantastically combining the letters in those names. Thus of the letters of Noah's name in Hebrew they made *Grace*, and of the Messiah's *He shall rejoice.* Whether the above origin be theoretical or not, the anagram can be

traced to the age of Lycophron, a Greek writer,
who flourished about 300 B.C.

Among the moderns, the French have most
cultivated the anagram. Camden says: "They
exceedingly admire the anagram, for the deep
and far-fetched antiquity and mystical meaning
therein. In the reign of Francis the First (when
learning began to revive), they began to distil
their wits therein." There is a curious anecdote
of an anagrammatist who presented a king of
France with the two following upon his name of
Bourbon:

Borbonius,	or	Borbonius,
Bonus orbi;		*Orbus boni;*

That is, "Bourbon good to the world;" or "Bourbon destitute of good;" while on another cele-
brated Frenchman we have—

Voltaire,
O alte vir.

Southey, in his "Doctor," says that "anagrams
are not likely ever again to hold so high a place
among the prevalent pursuits of literature as they
did in the seventeenth century. But no person," he
continues, "will ever hit upon an apt one without
feeling that degree of pleasure with which any odd

coincidence is remarked." In that century, indeed, the artifice appears to have become the fashionable literary passion of the day—the amusement of the learned and the wise, who sought

> " To purchase fame,
> In keen iambics and mild anagram."

While Andreas Rudiger was yet a student at college, and intending to become a physician, he one day pulled the Latinised form of his name to pieces, Andreas Rudigeras, and borrowing an *i*, transposed it into *Arare Rus Dei Dignus* ("Worthy to cultivate the land of God"). He fancied from this that he had a divine call to become an ecclesiastic, and thereupon gave up the study of medicine for theology. Soon after, Rudiger became tutor in the family of the philosopher Thomasius, who one day told him "that he would greatly benefit the journey of his life by turning it towards physic." Rudiger confessed that his tastes lay rather in that direction than to theology, but having looked upon the anagram of his name as an indication of a divine call, he had not dared to turn away from theology. "How simple you have been," replied Thomasius; "it is just that very anagram which calls you towards medicine—'*Rus Dei*,' the land

of God (God's acre), what is that but the cemetery
—and who labours so bravely for the cemetery as
a physician does?" Rudiger could not resist this,
returned to medicine, and became famous as a
physician.

An anagram on Monk, afterwards Duke of
Albemarle on the restoration of Charles II., forms
also a chronogram, including the date of the event
it records—

> Georgius Monke, Dux de Aumarle—
> *Ego Regem reduxi, anno sa* MDCLVV.

In this anagram the *c* takes the place of the *k*.

The old Puritan biographer, Cotton Mather,
claims for John Wilson—the subject of one of his
lives—the kingship of anagrammatising. "Of all
the anagrammatisers," he says in the third book
of his "Magnalia Christi Americana," "that have
been trying their fancies for the 2000 years that
have run out since the days of Lycophron, or the
more than 5000 since the days of our first father,
I believe there never was a man that made so
many, or so nimbly, as our Mr. Wilson; who,
together with his quick turns upon the names of
his friends, would ordinarily *fetch*, and rather than
lose, would even *force*, devout instructions out of

his anagrams. As one, upon hearing my father (Increase Mather) preach, Mr. Wilson immediately gave him that anagram upon his name 'Crescentius Matherus,' *En ! Christus Merces Tua* (Lo ! Christ is thy reward). There would scarcely occur the name of any remarkable person without an anagram raised thereupon."

This said John Wilson "forced instruction" out of his own name—first rendering it into Latin, Johannes Wilsonus, he found this anagram in it, "*In uno Jesu nos salvi*" (We are saved in one Jesus). This mode of Latinising names was common enough among those who liked this literary folly; thus we have Sir Robert Viner, or Robertus Vinerus, rendered "*Vir Bonus et Rarus*" (a good and rare man). The disciples of Descartes made a perfect anagram upon the Latinised name of their master, "Renatus Cartesius," one which not only takes up every letter, but which also expresses their opinion of that master's speciality—"*Tu scis res naturæ*" (Thou knowest the things of nature).

Pierre de St. Louis became a Carmelite monk on discovering that his name yielded a direction to that effect :

> Ludovicus Bartelemi—
> *Carmelo se devolvit.*

And, in the seventeenth century, André Pujom, finding that his name spelled *Pendu à Riom*, fulfilled his destiny by cutting somebody's throat in Auvergne, and was actually hung at Riom, the seat of justice in that province.

Occasionally when the anagram of a name did not make sense, there was added a rhyme to bring out a meaning. Thus, in a sermon preached by Dr. Edward Reynolds upon Peter Whalley, and entitled "Death's Advantage," every letter of the name is to be found in the first line of this verse:

> " *They reap well,*
> That Heaven obtain;
> Who sow like thee,
> Ne'er sow in vain."

In this sermon Peter Whalley is also anagrammatised into *A Whyte Perle*—this would not be a bad one, if orthography were of as little consequence as many of the old triflers in this way used to account it.

We read that when Alexander the Great was baffled before the walls of Tyre, and was about to raise the siege, he had a dream wherein he saw a satyr leaping about and trying to seize him. He consulted his sages, who read in the word Satyrus (the Greek for satyr), "*Sa Tyrus*"—"Tyre is thine!" Encouraged by this interpretation, Alexander made another assault and carried the city.

In a "New Help to Discourse" (London, 1684), there is one with a very quaint exposition:

TOAST—A SOTT.

> "A *toast* is like *a sot;* or what is most
> Comparative, *a sot* is like a *toast;*
> For when their substances in liquor sink,
> Both properly are said to be in drink."

It will be seen, however, that anagrams have chiefly been made upon proper names, and a reversing of their letters may sometimes pay the owner a compliment; as of the poet Waller:

> "His brows with laurel need not to be bound,
> Since in his *name* with *laurel* he is crowned."

George Thompson, the well-known anti-slavery advocate, was at one time solicited to go into parliament for the more efficient serving of the cause he had so much at heart. The question whether he would comply with this request or not was submitted to his friends, and one of them gave the following for answer:

George Thompson,
O go, the Negro's M.P.!

This clever instance was given in "Notes and Queries" a short time ago:

Thomas Carlyle,
A calm holy rest.

The following are additional instances.

Sir Francis Bacon, Lord Keeper—
Is born and elect for a rich speaker.

When, at the General Peace of 1814, Prussia absorbed a portion of Saxony, the king issued a new coinage of rix dollars, with their German name, *Ein Reichstahler*, impressed on them. The Saxons, by dividing the word, *Ein Reich stahl er*, made a sentence of which the meaning is, "He stole a kingdom!"

A good one is—

Henry John Templeton, Viscount Palmerston,
Only the Tiverton M.P. can help in our mess.

If we take from the words, *La Revolution Française*, the word *veto*, known as the first prerogative of Louis XIV., the remaining letters will form "*Un Corse la finira*"—*A Corsican shall end it*, and this may be regarded as an extraordinary coincidence, if nothing more. Many anagrams were made upon the name of Napoleon by superstitious persons, as—

Napoleon Bonaparte { *Bona rapta, leno, pone.*
{ *No, appear not at Elba.*

Louis Napoleon Bonaparte.
Arouse, Albion, an open plot.

A very apt anagram is the one founded upon—Sir
Edmundbury Godfrey, *I find murdered by rogues.*

EVIL.

" If you transpose what ladies wear,	*Veil.*
'Twill plainly show what bad folks are ;	*Vile.*
Again if you transpose the same,	
You'll see an ancient Hebrew name ;	*Levi.*
Change it again, and it will show	
What all on earth desire to do ;	*Live.*
Transpose the letters yet once more,	
What bad men do you'll then explore."	*Evil.*

The following are very apposite—

Sir Robert Peel,		Misanthrope,	
Terrible Poser.		*Spare him not.*	
Christianity,		Radical reform,	
It's in charity.		*Rare mad frolic.*	
Poorhouse,		Melodrama,	
O sour hope.		*Made moral.*	
Soldiers,		Arthur Wellesley,	
Lo! I dress.		*Truly he'll see war.*	
Notes and Queries,		The Field Marshall the Duke,	
A question sender.		*The Duke shall arm the field.*	
Solemnity,		Monarch,	
Yes, Milton.		*March on.*	
Determination,		Charades,	
I mean to rend it.		*Hard case.*	
Elegant,		David Livingstone,	
Neat leg.		*Go (D.V.) and visit the Nile.*	
Matrimony,		Stones.	
Into my arm.		*Notes.*	

THE ACROSTIC.

CROSTIC is the Greek name given to a poem the first letters of the lines in which taken together form a complete word or sentence, but most frequently a name. The invention of this kind of composition cannot be traced to any particular individual, but it is believed to have originated on the decline of pure classic literature. The early French poets, from the time of Francis I. to that of Louis XIV., practised it, but it was carried to its greatest perfection by the Elizabethan poets. Sir John Davies has no fewer than twenty-six poems entitled "Hymns to Astræa," every one of which is an acrostic on the words, "Elizabetha Regina." Traces of something akin are to be found in the poetry of the Jews,—for example, the 119th Psalm,—and also in the Greek "Anthology." Here it may be noted that in Greek the word *Adam* is compounded of the initial letters of the four cardinal points:

Arktos   = north,
Dusis   = west,
Anatolê   = east,
Mesembria   = south ;

and that the Hebrew word, ADM forms the
acrostic of A[dam], D[avid], M[essiah].

It is hardly necessary to give many specimens
of this kind of literary composition in these days,
since there are so many periodicals continually
giving acrostics and relative verses, and a very few
instances may suffice. The following old verses
were originally written in a copy of Parkhurst's
poems presented by the author to Thomas Buttes,
who himself wrote this acrostic on his own name:

" *T*he longer lyfe that man on earth enjoyes,
  *H*is God so much the more hee dooth offende ;
  *O*ffending God, no doubt, mannes soule destroyes ;
  *M*annes soule destroyed, his torments have no ende ;
  *A*nd endles torments sinners must endure,
  *S*ith synne Gods wrath agaynst us doth procure.

  *B*eware, therefore, O wretched sinfull Wight,
  *U*se well thy toongue, doo well, think not amysse ;
  *T*o God praye thou to guyde thee by his spright,
  *T*hat thou mayest treade the path of perfect blisse.
  *E*mbrace thou Christe, by faythe and fervent love,
  *S*o shalt thou reyne with hym in heaven above.

Thomas Buttes
> havying the first letter of everie lyne
> begynnyng with a letter of his name. "

A Song of Rejoysing for the Prosperous Reigne
  of our most Gratious Soveraigne Lady, Queene
  Elizabeth.

" G   Geve laude unto the Lorde,
        And prayse His holy name
  O   O let us all with one accorde
        Now magnifie the same
  D   Due thanks unto Him yeeld
        Who evermore hath beene
  S   So strong defence buckler and shielde
        To our most Royall Queene.

  A   And as for her this daie
        Each where about us rounde
  V   Up to the skie right solemnelie
        The bells doe make a sounde
  E   Even so let us rejoice
        Before the Lord our King
  T   To him let us now frame our voyce
        With chearefull hearts to sing.

  H   Her Majesties intent
        By thy good grace and will
  E   Ever O Lorde hath bene most bent
        Thy lawe for to fulfil

Q   Quite Thou that loving minde
    With love to her agayne
U   Unto her as Thou hast beene kinde
    O Lord so still remaine.

E   Extende Thy mightie hand
    Against her mortall foes
E   Expresse and shewe that Thou wilt stand
    With her against all those
N   Nigh unto her abide
    Upholde her scepter strong
E   Eke graunt us with a joyfull guide
    She may continue long.

                              Amen. "

The next is from Planché's "Songs and Poems:"

To Beatrice.

" *B*eauty to claim, amongst the fairest place,
  *E*nchanting manner, unaffected grace,
  *A*rch without malice, merry but still wise,
  *T*ruth ever on her lips as in her eyes ;
  *R*eticent not from sullenness or pride,
  *I*ntensity of feeling but to hide ;
  *C*an any doubt such being there may be ?
  *E*ach line I pen, points, matchless maid, to thee ! "

Mdlle. Rachel was the recipient of the most delicate compliment the acrostic has ever been employed to convey. A diadem was presented to her, so arranged that the initial of the name of each

stone was also the initial of one of her principal
rôles, and in their order formed her name—

*R*uby,	*R*oxana,
*A*methyst,	*A*menaide,
Cornelian,	Camille,
*H*ematite,	*H*ermione,
*E*merald,	*E*milie,
*L*apis lazuli,	*L*aodice.

The following is an ingenious combination of
acrostic and telestic combined :

" *U*nite and untie are the same—so say yo*u*
*N*ot in wedlock, I ween, has the unity bee*n*
*I*n the drama of marriage, each wandering gou*t*
*T*o a new face would fly—all except you and *I*
*E*ach seeking to alter the *spell* in their scen*e*."

Edgar A. Poe was the author of a complicated
poem of this class, in which the first letter in the
lady's name is the first in the first line ; the second,
second in the second line ; the third, third in the
third line, and so on—

A VALENTINE.
(*Frances Sargent Osgood.*)

" For her this rhyme is penned, whose luminous eyes,
  Brightly expressive as the twins of Leda,
  Shall find her own sweet name, that nestling lies
  Upon the page, enwrapped from every reader.

Search narrowly the lines !—they hold a treasure
Divine—a talisman—an amulet
That must be worn *at heart.* Search well the measure—
The words—the syllables ! Do not forget
The trivialest point, or you may lose your labour !
And yet there is in this no Gordian knot
Which one might not undo without a sabre,
If one could merely comprehend the plot.
Enwritten upon the leaf where now are peering
Eye's scintillating soul, there lie *perdus*
Three eloquent words oft uttered in the hearing
Of poets by poets—as the name is a poet's, too,
Its letters, although naturally lying
Like the Knight Pinto—Mendez Ferdinando—
Still form a synonym for Truth. Cease trying !
You will not read the riddle, though you do the best
    you *can* do ! "

ALLITERATIVE AND ALPHABETIC VERSE.

HERE are some clever lines which illustrate this style on the Bunker Hill Monument celebration :

"Americans arrayed and armed attend :
Beside battalions bold, bright beauties blend,
Chiefs, clergy, citizens, conglomerate,—
Detesting despots,—daring deeds debate ;
Each eye emblazoned ensigns entertain,—
Flourishing from far, fan freedom's flame.
Guards greeting guards grown gray,—guest greeting
    guest.
High-minded heroes hither homeward haste,
Ingenuous juniors join in jubilee,
Kith kenning kin, kind knowing kindred key.
Lo, lengthened lines lend Liberty liege love,
Mixed masses, marshalled, Monumentward move.
Note noble navies near—no novel notion
Oft our oppressors overawed old Ocean ;

Presumptuous princes pristine patriots paled,
Queen's quarrel questing quotas, quondam quailed.
Rebellion roused, revolting ramparts rose.
Stout spirits, smiting servile soldiers, strove.
These thrilling themes, to thousands truly told,
Usurpers' unjust usages unfold.
Victorious vassals, vauntings vainly veiled,
Where, whilesince, Webster warlike Warren wailed.
'Xcuse 'xpletives, 'xtra queer 'xpressed,
Yielding Yankee yeomen Zest."

PRINCE CHARLES AFTER CULLODEN.

" All ardent acts affright an age abased
By brutal broils, by braggart bravery braced.
Craft's cankered courage changed Culloden's cry ;
' Deal deep' deposed ' deal death '—' decoy '—' defy ! '
Enough.   Ere envy enters England's eyes,
Fancy's false future fades, for Fortune flies.
Gaunt, gloomy, guarded, grappling giant griefs,
Here hunted hard, his harassed heart he heaves ;
In impious ire incessant ills invests,
Judging Jove's jealous judgments, jaundiced jests !
Kneel kirtled knight ! keep keener kingcraft known,
Let larger lore life's levelling lesson's loan ;
Marauders must meet malefactors' meeds.
No nation noisy nonconformists needs.
O, oracles of old ! our orb ordain
Peace's possession—Plenty's palmy plain !

Quiet Quixotic quests; quell quarrelling;
Rebuke red riot's resonant rifle ring.
Slumber seems strangely sweet since silence smote
The threatening thunders throbbing through their
  throat.
Usurper! under uniform unwont
Vail valour's vaguest venture, vainest vaunt.
Well wot we which were wise.   War's wildfire won
Ximenes, Xerxes, Xavier, Xenophon :
Yet you, ye yearning youth, your young years yield
Zuinglius' zealous zest—Zinzendorf Zion-zealed."

An Animal Alphabet.

" Alligator, beetle, porcupine, whale,
  Bobolink, panther, dragon-fly, snail,
  Crocodile, monkey, buffalo, hare,
  Dromedary, leopard, mud-turtle, bear,
  Elephant, badger, pelican, ox,
  Flying-fish, reindeer, anaconda, fox,
  Guinea-pig, dolphin, antelope, goose,
  Humming-bird, weasel, pickerel, moose,
  Ibex, rhinoceros, owl, kangaroo,
  Jackal, opossum, toad, cockatoo,
  Kingfisher, peacock, anteater, bat,
  Lizard, ichneumon, honey-bee, rat,
  Mocking-bird, camel, grasshopper, mouse,
  Nightingale, spider, cuttle-fish, grouse,
  Ocelot, pheasant, wolverine, auk,
  Periwinkle, ermine, katydid, hawk,

> Quail, hippopotamus, armadillo, **moth**,
> Rattlesnake, lion, woodpecker, **sloth**,
> **Salamander**, goldfinch, angleworm, dog,
> Tiger, flamingo, scorpion, frog,
> **Unicorn**, ostrich, nautilus, mole,
> **Viper**, gorilla, basilisk, sole,
> Whippoorwill, **beaver**, **centipede**, **fawn**,
> **Xantho**, canary, polliwog, swan,
> Yellowhammer, **eagle**, hyena, lark,
> Zebra, chameleon, butterfly, **shark**."

Of affected alliteration as used by modern poets, there is a very good imitation of Swinburne's style in Bayard Taylor's "Diversions of the Echo Club,"* where Galahad chants "in rare and rhythmic redundancy, the viciousness of virtue:"

THE LAY OF MACARONI.

" As a wave that steals when the winds are stormy
  From creek to cove of the curving shore,
Buffeted, blown, and broken before me,
  Scattered and spread to its sunlit core.
As a dove that dips in the dark of maples,
  To sip the sweetness of shelter and shade,
I kneel in thy nimbus, O noon of Naples,
  I bathe in thine beauty, by thee embayed.

What is it ails me that I should sing of her?
  The queen of the flashes and flames that were!

* Chatto and Windus, London.

Yea, I have felt the shuddering sting of her,
　The flower-sweet throat and the hands of her !
I have swayed and sung to the sound of her psalters,
　I have danced her dances of dizzy delight,
I have hallowed mine hair to the horns of her altars,
　Between the nightingale's song and the night !

What is it, Queen, that now I should do for thee ?
　What is it now I should ask at thine hands?
Blow of the trumpets thine children once blew for thee
　Break from thine feet and thine bosom the bands?
Nay, as sweet as the songs of Leone Leoni,
　And gay as her garments of gem-sprinkled gold,
She gives me mellifluous, mild macaroni,
　The choice of her children when cheeses are old !

And over me hover, as if by the wings of it,
　Frayed in the furnace by flame that is fleet,
The curious coils and the strenuous strings of it,
　Dropping, diminishing down, as I eat ;
Lo ! and the beautiful Queen, as she brings of it,
　Lifts me the links of the limitless chain,
Bidding mine mouth chant the splendidest things of it,
　Out of the wealth of my wonderful brain !

Behold ! I have done it ; my stomach is smitten
　With sweets of the surfeit her hands have enrolled.
Italia, mine cheeks with thine kisses are bitten :
　I am broken with beauty, stabbed, slaughtered, and
　　　sold !

No man of thy millions is more macaronied,
  Save mighty Mazzini, than musical Me :
The souls of the Ages shall stand as astonied,
  And faint in the flame I am fanning for thee!"

The above reminds of the anecdote told of Mrs.
Crawford, who is said to have written one line of
her "Kathleen Mavourneen," on purpose to confound the Cockney warblers, who would sing it—

"The 'orn of the 'unter is 'eard on the 'ill ;"

and again, in Moore's "Ballad Stanzas":

  "If there's peace to be found in the world,
A 'eart that was 'umble might 'ope for it 'ere ! "

Or—

  "Ha helephant heasily heats hat his hease
  Hunder humbrageous humbrella trees ! "

In the number of "Society" for April 23, 1881,
there appeared several excellent specimens of alliterative verse, in compliance with a competition
instituted by that paper for certain prizes—the
selected verses all begin with the letter *b* :

"Bloom, beauteous blossoms, budding bowers beneath !
  Behold, Boreas' bitter blast by brief
Bright beams becalmed ; balmy breezes breathe,
  Banishing blight, bring bliss beyond belief.

Build, bonny birds ! By bending birchen bough,
  By bush, by beech, by buttressed branches bare,

By bluebell-brightened bramble-brake ; bestow
  Bespeckled broods ; but bold bad boys beware !

Babble, blithe brooklet !   Barren borders breach,
  Bathe broomy banks, bright buttercups bedew,
Briskly by bridge, by beetling bluff, by beach,
  Beckoned by bravely bounding billows blue ! ”
                              —*Sir Patrick Fells.*

    “ Brimming brooklets bubble,
        Buoyant breezes blow,
      Baby-billows breaking
        Bashfully below.

      Blossom-burdened branches,
        Briared banks betide,
      Bright bewitching bluebells
        Blooming bend beside.

      But beyond be breakers,
        Bare blasts brooding black,
      Bitterly bemoaning
        Broken barks borne back.”
                              —*A. M. Morgan.*

    “ Beverage by bibbers blest,
        Balmy beer—bewitching bane,
      British brewings, boasted best,
        Blunting Bacchus’ brandied brain.
      Bonny bumpers brimmed by beads,
        Barley-born, bring blind relief,
      Bubbling Bass-brewed Burton breed
        Bland beguilement, bright but brief.

Bar-bought beer—bah ! bitter brine—
Barrel-broaching braves, beware !
Bid Bavaria, benign,
Better brews bold Britons bear." '

—*W. H. Evans.*

Mr. Swinburne, of whose style there has been given an imitation, is not the only poet who is prone to alliteration—in fact, all poets are given more or less to it, though not to the same extent. When used excessively it is as disagreeable as any other excess, yet its occasional use unquestionably adds to grace and style.

Pope says on this point in the following lines, which are also alliterative—

"'Tis not enough no harshness gives offence,
The sound must seem an echo to the sense.
Soft is the strain when zephyr gently blows,
And the smooth stream in smoother numbers flows ;
But when loud surges lash the sounding shore,
The hoarse rough verse should like the torrent roar."

We find this example in Tennyson :

" The splendour falls on castle walls,
And snowy summits old in story ;
The long light shakes across the lakes,
And the wild cataract leaps in glory.
Blow, bugle, blow, set the wild echoes flying ;
Blow, bugle ; answer, echoes, dying, dying, dying."

Crabbe also used this ornament profusely, as :

" Then 'cross the bounding brook they make their way
O'er its rough bridge, and there behold the bay ;
The ocean smiling to the fervid sun,
The waves that faintly fall and slowly run,
The ships at distance, and the boats at hand,
And now they walk upon the seaside sand,
Counting the number, and what kind they be,
Ships softly sinking in the sleepy sea."

Take also this from Shelley's "Ode to a Sky-lark : "

" Teach me half the gladness
That my brain must know,
Such harmonious madness
From my lips would flow,
The world should listen then, as I am listening now.

.   .   .   .   .   .

Waking or asleep,
Thou of death must deem
Things more true and deep
Than we mortals dream,
Or how could thy notes flow in such a crystal stream ? "

In the numbers of " Truth " for November 1881, there appeared a variety of excellent examples of alphabetic verses in the course of a competition, and of these there follows one:

A Yacht Alphabet.

"A was the Anchor which held fast our ship;

B was the Boatswain, with whistle to lip;

C was the Captain, who took the command;

D was the Doctor, with physic at hand;

E was the Euchre we played on the quiet;

F was the Fellow who kicked up a riot;

G was the Girl who was always so ill;

H was the Hammock from which I'd a spill;

I was the Iceberg we passed on our way;

J was the Jersey I wore all the day;

K was the Keel, which was stuck on the shore;

L was the Lubber we all thought a bore;

M was the Mate, no one better I'd wish;

N was the Net in which I caught a fish;

O was the Oar which I broke—'twas so weak;

P was the Pennon which flew at our peak;

Q was the Quoit which was made out of rope;

R was the Rat which would eat all our soap;

S was the Sailor who got very tight;

T was the Tempest which came on one night;

U was the Uproar the night of the storm;

V was the Vessel we spoke in due form;

W's the Watch which the crew kept in turn;

X was Xantippe, whom each one did spurn;

Y was our Yacht, which flew through the foam;

Z was the Zany who wouldn't leave home."

NONSENSE VERSE.

HE following lines have been kindly sent us by Professor E. H. Palmer, who wrote them after a cruise on a friend's yacht, and are an abortive attempt to get up a knowledge of nautical terms.

THE SHIPWRECK.

" Upon the poop the captain stands,
 As starboard as may be ;
And pipes on deck the topsail hands
To reef the top-sail-gallant strands
 Across the briny sea.

' Ho ! splice the anchor under-weigh !
 The captain loudly cried ;
' Ho ! lubbers brave, belay ! belay !
For we must luff for Falmouth Bay
 Before to-morrow's tide.'

The good ship was a racing yawl,
 A spare-rigged schooner sloop,
Athwart the bows the taffrails all
In grummets gay appeared to fall,
 To deck the mainsail poop.

But ere they made the Foreland Light,
    And Deal was left behind ;
The wind it blew great gales that night,
And blew the doughty captain tight,
    Full three sheets in the wind.

And right across the tiller head
    The horse it ran apace,
Whereon a traveller hitched and sped
Along the jib and vanishéd
    To heave the trysail brace.

What ship could live in such a sea !
    What vessel bear the shock ?
' Ho ! starboard port your helm-a-lee !
Ho ! reef the maintop-gallant-tree,
    With many a running block !'

And right upon the Scilly Isles
    The ship had run aground ;
When lo ! the stalwart Captain Giles
Mounts up upon the gaff and smiles,
    And slews the compass round.

'Saved ! saved !' with joy the sailors cry,
    And scandalise the skiff ;
As taut and hoisted high and dry
They see the ship unstoppered lie
    Upon the sea-girt cliff.

And since that day in Falmouth Bay,
    As herring-fishers trawl,

The younkers hear the boatswains say
How Captain Giles that awful day
　　Preserved the sinking yawl."

Mr. Charles G. Leland sends the following, with the remark that he thinks the lines "the finest and daintiest nonsense" he ever read:

"Thy heart is like some icy lake,
　On whose cold brink I stand;
Oh, buckle on my spirit's skate,
And lead, thou living saint, the way
　To where the ice is thin—
That it may break beneath my feet
　And let a lover in!"

A short time ago in the new series of *Household Words*, a prize was offered for the writing of Nonsense Verses of eight lines. Of the lines sent in by the competitors we give three specimens:

"How many strive to force a way
Where none can go save those who pay,
To verdant plains of soft delight
The homage of the silent night,
When countless stars from pole to pole
Around the earth unceasing roll
In roseate shadow's silvery hue,
Shine forth and gild the morning dew."

　　　　　　　　　　　　　　—Arym.

"And must we really part for good,
But meet again here where we've stood?

No more delightful trysting-place,
We've watched sweet Nature's smiling face.
No more the landscape's lovely brow,
Exchange our mutual breathing vow.
Then should the twilight draw around
No loving interchange of sound."

—Culver.

" Less for renown than innate love,
These to my wish must recreant prove ;
Nor whilst an impulse here remain,
Can ever hope the soul to gain ;
For memory scanning all the past,
Relaxes her firm bonds at last,
And gives to candour all the grace
The heart can in its temple trace."

—Dum Spiro Spero.

The curious style of some versifiers has been well
imitated in the following

BALLAD OF THE PERIOD.

" An auld wife sat at her ivied door
    (*Butter and eggs and a pound of cheese*) ;
A thing she had frequently done before ;
    And her knitting reposed on her aproned knees.

The piper he piped on the hill-top high
    (*Butter and eggs and a pound of cheese*) ;
Till the cow said, 'I die,' and the goose said, 'Why?'
    And the dog said nothing but searched for fleas.

.   .   .   .   .

The farmer's daughter hath soft brown hair
　　(*Butter and eggs and a pound of cheese*);
And I've met a ballad, I can't tell where,
　　Which mainly consisted of lines like these."

W. S. Gilbert has some verses which are true nonsense, of which this is one:

"Sing for the garish eye,
　　When moonless brandlings cling!
Let the froddering crooner cry,
　　And the braddled sapster sing.
For never and never again,
　　Will the tottering beechlings play,
For bratticed wrackers are singing aloud,
　　And the throngers croon in May!"

Mr. Lewis Carroll's "Hunting of the Snark"* is a very curious little book, full of the most delicate fun and queer nonsense, with delightful illustrations. It gives an account of how a Bell-man, Boots, Barrister, Broker, Billiard-marker, Banker, Beaver, Baker, and Butcher go a-hunting after a mythical Beast called a "Snark." It is difficult to detach a passage for quotation, but the following few lines will show how the "Quest of the Snark" was purposed to be carried on:

"To seek it with thimbles, to seek it with care:
　　To pursue it with forks and hope;

* Macmillan & Co., London.

To threaten its life with a railway share ;
 To charm it with smiles and soap !

For the Snark's a peculiar creature, that won't
 Be caught in a commonplace way ;
Do all that you know, and try all that you don't :
 Not a chance must be wasted to-day ! "

The verses which follow are from the "Comic Latin Grammar," and if they are not nonsense they show at least how thin the partition line is between true nonsense verse and many of those pieces which were wont to be known by the name of Album Verses :

LINES BY A FOND LOVER.

" Lovely maid, with rapture swelling,
 Should these pages meet thine eye,
Clouds of absence soft dispelling ;—
 Vacant memory heaves a sigh.

As the rose, with fragrance weeping,
 Trembles to the tuneful wave,
So my heart shall twine unsleeping,
 Till it canopies the grave.

Though another's smile's requited,
 Envious fate my doom should be ;
Joy for ever disunited,
 Think, ah ! think, at times on me !

Oft, amid the spicy gloaming,
 Where the brakes their songs instil,

Fond affection silent roaming,
　　Loves to linger by the rill—

There, when echo's voice consoling,
　　Hears the nightingale complain,
Gentle sighs my lips controlling,
　　Bind my soul in beauty's chain.

Oft in slumber's deep recesses,
　　I thy mirror'd image see;
Fancy mocks the vain caresses
　　I would lavish like a bee!

But how vain is glittering sadness!
　　Hark, I hear distraction's knell!
Torture gilds my heart with madness!
　　Now for ever fare thee well!"

LIPOGRAMS.

THE reading of Lope de Vega's five novels, in each of which a different vowel is omitted, led to Lord Holland writing the following curious production, in which no vowel is used but *e:*

EVE'S LEGEND.

" Men were never perfect; yet the three brethren Veres were ever esteemed, respected, revered, even when the rest, whether the select few, whether the mere herd, were left neglected.

"The eldest's vessels seek the deep, stem the element, get pence; the keen Peter when free, wedded Hester Green,—the slender, stern, severe, erect Hester Green. The next, clever Ned, less dependent, wedded sweet Ellen Heber. Stephen, ere he met the gentle Eve, never felt tenderness: he kept kennels, bred steeds, rested where the deer fed, went where green trees, where fresh breezes greeted sleep. There he met the meek, the gentle Eve; she tended her sheep, she ever neglected self; she never heeded pelf, yet she heeded the shepherds even less. Nevertheless, her cheek reddened when she met Stephen; yet decent reserve, meek respect, tempered her speech, even when she showed tenderness. Stephen felt the sweet effect: he felt he erred when he fled the sex, yet felt he defenceless when Eve seemed tender. She, he reflects, never deserved neglect; she never vented spleen; he esteems her gentleness, her endless deserts; he reverences her steps; he greets her:

"'Tell me whence these meek, these gentle sheep,— whence the yet meeker, the gentler shepherdess?'

"'Well bred, we were eke better fed, ere we went where reckless men seek fleeces. There we were fleeced. Need then rendered me shepherdess, need renders me sempstress. See me tend the sheep, see me sew the wretched shreds. Eve's need preserves the steers, preserves the sheep; Eve's needle mends her dresses, hems her sheets; Eve feeds the geese; Eve preserves the cheese.'

"Her speech melted Stephen, yet he nevertheless esteems, reveres her. He bent the knee where her feet pressed the green ; he blessed, he begged, he pressed her.

" ' Sweet, sweet Eve, let me wed thee ; be led where Hester Green, where Ellen Heber, where the brethren Vere dwell. Free cheer greets thee there ; Ellen's glees sweeten the refreshments ; there severer Hester's decent reserve checks heedless jests. Be led there, sweet Eve.'

" ' Never! we well remember the Seer. We went where he dwells—we entered the cell—we begged the decree,—

" ' Where, whenever, when, 'twere well
Eve be wedded ? Eld Seer, tell !

" ' He rendered the decree ; see here the sentence decreed !' Then she presented Stephen the Seer's decree. The verses were these :

" ' *Ere the green be red,*
Sweet Eve, be never wed ;
Ere be green the red cheek,
Never wed thee, Eve meek.'

"The terms perplexed Stephen, yet he jeered them. He resented the senseless credence, ' Seers never err.' Then he repented, knelt, wheedled, wept. Eve sees Stephen kneel, she relents, yet frets when she remembers the Seer's decree. Her dress redeems her. These were the events :

" Her well-kempt tresses fell : sedges, reeds beckoned them. The reeds fell, the edges met her cheeks ; her cheeks bled. She presses the green sedge where her cheek bleeds. Red then bedewed the green reed, the green reed then speckled her red cheek. The red cheek seems green, the green reed seems red. These were the terms the Eld Seer decreed Stephen Vere.

HERE ENDETH THE LEGEND."

The following curious lines run in quite an opposite way to the preceding, for each verse has been written so as to include every letter in the alphabet but the vowel *e :*

THE FATE OF NASSAN.

" Bold Nassan quits his caravan,
    A hazy mountain grot to scan ;
    Climbs jaggy rocks to spy his way,
    Doth tax his sight, but far doth stray.

    Not work of man, nor sport of child,
    Finds Nassan in that mazy wild ;
    Lax grows his joints, limbs toil in vain—
    Poor wight ! why didst thou quit that plain

    Vainly for succour Nassan calls,
    Know, Zillah, that thy Nassan falls ;
    But prowling wolf and fox may joy,
    To quarry on thy Arab boy."

Here follows a fugitive verse, written with *ease* without *e's :*

    " A jovial swain may rack his brain,
        And tax his fancy's might,
      To quiz in vain, for 'tis most plain,
        That what I say is right."

CENTONES OR MOSAICS.

F this formerly favourite amusement of the learned we give several examples, only noting here that the word "Cento" primarily signified a cloak made of patches.

1. I only knew she came and went,
2.   Like troutlets in a pool;
3. She was a phantom of delight,
4.   And I was like a fool.

5. One kiss, dear maid, I said, and sighed,
6.   Out of those lips unshorn,
7. She shook her ringlets round her head
8.   And laughed in merry scorn.

9. Ring out, wild bells, to the wild sky,
10.   You heard them, O my heart;
11. 'Tis twelve at night by the castle clock,
12.   Beloved, we must part.

13. "Come back, come back!" she cried in grief,
14.   My eyes are dim with tears—
15. How shall I live through all the days?
16.   All through a hundred years?

17. 'Twas in the prime of summer time,
18.   She blessed me with her hand;

19. We strayed together, deeply blest,
20.   Into the dreaming land.

21. The laughing bridal roses blow,
22.   To dress her dark-brown hair;
23. My heart is breaking with my woe,
24.   Most beautiful! most rare!

25. I clasped it on her sweet, cold hand,
26.   The precious golden link!
27. I calmed her fears, and she was calm,
28.   "Drink, pretty creature, drink!"

29. And so I won my Genevieve,
30.   And walked in Paradise;
31. The fairest thing that ever grew
32.   Atween me and the skies!

1. Powell; 2. Hood; 3. Wordsworth; 4. Eastman; 5. Coleridge; 6. Longfellow; 7. Stoddard; 8. Tennyson; 9. Tennyson; 10. Alice Cary; 11. Coleridge; 12. Alice Cary; 13. Campbell; 14. Bayard Taylor; 15. Osgood; 16. T. S. Perry; 17. Hood; 18. Hoyt; 19. Edwards; 20. Cornwall; 21. Patmore; 22. Bayard Taylor; 23. Tennyson; 24. Read; 25. Browning; 26. Smith; 27. Coleridge; 28. Wordsworth; 29. Coleridge; 30. Hervey; 31. Wordsworth; 32. Osgood.

The next appeared a short time ago in one of the Edinburgh newspapers, signed R. Fleming, and is a mosaic compilation from poems written to the memory of Robert Burns:

1. Immortal bard, immortal Burns!
2.   Whose lines are mottoes of the heart;
3. Affection loves and memory learns
4.   Thy songs "untaught by rules of art."

5. For dear as life—as heaven—will be,
6. 　　As years on years successive roll;
7. Fair types of thy rich harmony
8. 　　Who wrote to humanise the soul.

9. His lyre was sweet, majestic, grand,
10. 　　The pride and honour of the North;
11. His song was of bold freedom's land,
12. 　　Brave Scotland, freedom's throne on earth.

13. Oft by the winding banks of Ayr;
14. 　　With sinewy arm he turned the soil;
15. He painted Scotland's daughters fair,
16. 　　Through twilight shades of good and ill.

17. His native wild enchanting strains,
18. 　　Like dear memories round the hearth,
19. Immortalise the poet's name,
20. 　　And few have won a greener wreath.

21. From John O'Groat's to 'cross the Tweed
22. 　　What heart hath ever matched his flame?
23. Though rough and dark the path he trod,
24. 　　Long shall old Scotland keep his name.

25. Great master of our Doric rhyme,
26. 　　Though here thy course was but a span;
27. The pealing rapturous notes sublime
28. 　　Binds man with fellow-man.

29. Peace to the dead—in Scotia's choir—
30. 　　Yes, future bards shall pour the lay,
31. Warmed with a "spark of nature's fire,"
32. 　　While years insidious steal away.

1. Bennoch ; 2. Campbell ; 3. Imlach ; 4. Gray ; 5. Glen ; 6. Paul ; 7. M'Laggan ; 8. Tannahill ; 9. Glen ; 10. Allan ; 11. Gilfillan ; 12. Park ; 13. Wallace ; 14. Roscoe ; 15. Vedder ; 16. Wordsworth ; 17. Reid ; 18. Glass ; 19. Paul ; 20. Halleck ; 21. Macindoe ; 22. Ainslie ; 23. Halleck ; 24. Kelly ; 25. Gray ; 26. Mercer ; 27. Vedder ; 28. Imlach ; 29. Montgomery ; 30. Gray ; 31. Rushton ; 32. Gilfillan.

The three following verses are very good :

1. When first I met thee, warm and young,
2.   My heart I gave thee with my hand ;
3. My name was then a magic spell,
4.   Casting a dim religious light.

5. But now, as we plod on our way,
6.   My heart no more with rapture swells ;
7. I would not, if I could, be gay,
8.   When earth is filled with cold farewells !

9. The heath this night must be my bed,
10.   Ye vales, ye streams, ye groves, adieu ?
11. Farewell for aye, e'en love is dead,
12.   Would I could add, remembrance too !

1. Moore ; 2. Morris ; 3. Norton ; 4. Milton ; 5. Percival ; 6. M'Naughton ; 7. Rogers ; 8. Patmore ; 9. Scott ; 10. Pope ; 11. Procter ; 12. Byron.

The following is copied from " Fireside Amusements," published by the Messrs. Chambers, every line being taken from a different poet :

" On Linden when the sun was low,
   A frog he would a-wooing go ;
   He sighed a sigh, and breathed a prayer,
   None but the brave deserve the fair.

A gentle knight was pricking o'er the plain,
Remote, unfriended, melancholy, slow;
Gums and pomatums shall his flight restrain,
Or who would suffer being here below.

The younger of the sister arts
Was born on the open sea;
The rest were slain at Chevy Chase,
Under the greenwood tree.

At morn the blackcock trims his jetty wings,
And says—remembrance saddening o'er each brow—
Awake, my St. John! leave all meaner things!
Who would be free themselves must strike the blow!

It was a friar of orders gray,
Still harping on my daughter:
Sister spirit, come away,
Across this stormy water.

On the light fantastic toe,
Othello's occupation's gone;
Maid of Athens, ere I go,
Were the last words of Marmion.

There was a sound of revelry by night
In Thebes' streets three thousand years ago;
And comely virgins came with garlands dight
To censure Fate, and pious Hope forgo.

Oh! the young Lochinvar came out of the west,
An underbred fine-spoken fellow was he;
A back dropping in, an expansion of chest,
Far more than I once could foresee."

ECHO VERSES.

A Gentle Echo on Woman.

(IN THE DORIC MANNER.)

Shepherd. Echo, I ween, will in the woods reply,
        And quaintly answer questions : shall I try?
Echo.   Try.
Shep. What must we do our passion to express?
Echo.   Press.
Shep. How shall I please her, who ne'er loved before?
Echo.   Before.
Shep. What most moves women when we them address?
Echo.   A dress.
Shep. Say, what can keep her chaste whom I adore?
Echo.   A door.
Shep. If music softens rocks, love tunes my lyre.
Echo.   Liar.
Shep. Then teach me, Echo, how shall I come by her?
Echo.   Buy her.
Shep. When bought, no question I shall be her dear?
Echo.   Her dear.
Shep. But deer have horns : how must I keep her under?
Echo.   Keep her under.
Shep. But what can glad me when she's laid on bier?
Echo.   Beer.
Shep. What must I do when women will be kind?
Echo.   Be kind.
Shep. What must I do when women will be cross?
Echo.   Be cross.

Shep. Lord, what is she that can so turn and wind?
Echo.   Wind.
Shep. If she be wind, what stills her when she blows?
Echo.   Blows.
Shep. But if she bang again, still should I bang her?
Echo.   Bang her.
Shep. Is there no way to moderate her anger?
Echo.   Hang her.
Shep. Thanks, gentle Echo! right thy answers tell
        What woman is and how to guard her well.
Echo.   Guard her well.

ECHO AND THE LOVER.

Lover. Echo! mysterious nymph, declare
        Of what you're made, and what you are.
Echo.   Air.
Lover. 'Mid airy cliffs and places high,
        Sweet Echo! listening love, you lie.
Echo.   You lie.
Lover. Thou dost resuscitate dead sounds—
        Hark! how my voice revives, resounds!
Echo.   Zounds!
Lover. I'll question thee before I go—
        Come, answer me more apropos!
Echo.   Poh! Poh!
Lover. Tell me, fair nymph, if ere you saw
        So sweet a girl as Phœbe Shaw?
Echo.   Pshaw!
Lover. Say what will turn that frisking coney
        Into the toils of matrimony?
Echo.   Money!
Lover. Has Phœbe not a heavenly brow?
        Is not her bosom white as snow?
Echo.   Ass! no!

Lover. Her eyes ! was ever such a pair ?
      Are the stars brighter than they are.
Echo.   They are.
Lover. Echo, thou liest ! but canst deceive me.
Echo.   Leave me.
Lover. But come, thou saucy, pert romancer,
      Who is as fair as Phœbe ? Answer !
Echo.   Ann, sir

The latest good verses of this class are attributed
to an echo that haunts the Sultan's palace at Con-
stantinople. Abdul Hamid is supposed to question
it as to the intentions of the European powers and
his own resources :

      " L'Angleterre ?
             Erre.
     L'Autriche ?
             Triche.
     La Prusse ?
             Russe.
   Mes principautés ?
             Otées.
   Mes cuirasses ?
             Assez.
   Mes Pashas ?
             Achats.
   Et Suleiman ?
             Ment."
                —*The Athenæum.*

WATCH-CASE VERSES.

HEN thick watches with removable cases were in fashion, and before the introduction of the present compact form, the outer case of the old-fashioned "turnip" was frequently the repository of verses and sundry devices, generally placed there by the watchmaker. Others, again, consisted of the maker's name and address, with some appropriate maxim, and were printed on satin or worked with the needle, and occasionally so devised as to appear in a circle without a break, as in the following :

> " Onward
> perpetually moving
> These faithful hands are proving
> How soft the hours steal by ;
> This monitory pulse-like beating,
> Is oftentimes methinks repeating,
> ' Swift, swift, the hours do fly.'
> Ready ! be ready ! perhaps before
> These hands have made
> One revolution more,
> Life's spring is snapt,—
> You die ! "

A watch-paper described by a writer in "Notes and Queries" gave the address of Bowen, 2 Tichborne Street, Piccadilly, on a pedestal surmounted by an urn. On the other side of the label was a winged figure, holding in one hand a watch at arm's length, and in the other a book. At her feet lay a sickle and a serpent with his tail in his mouth —the emblems of Time and Eternity. Round the circumference of the label were these lines—

> " Little monitor, impart
> Some instruction to the heart;
> Show the busy and the gay
> Life is wasting swift away.
> Follies cannot long endure,
> Life is short and death is sure.
> Happy those who wisely learn
> Truth from error to discern :
> Truth, immortal as the soul,
> And unshaken as the pole."

The bottom of the case was lined with rose-coloured satin, on which was a device in lace-paper —the central portion representing two hearts transfixed by arrows, and surmounted by a dove holding a wreath in its bill. A circular band enclosed the device, and bore the motto—

> " Joined by friendship,
> Crowned by love."

The lines next given are by Mr. J. Byrom, common called Dr. Byrom, whom we have previously referred to :

"Could but our tempers move like this machine,
  Not urged by passion, nor delayed by spleen ;
  But true to Nature's regulating power,
  By virtuous acts distinguish every hour :
  Then health and joy would follow, as they ought,
  The laws of motion and the laws of thought :
  On earth would pass the pleasant moments o'er
  To rest in Heaven when Time shall be no more !"

The last lines of this watch-paper have been occasionally varied to—

"Sweet health to pass the pleasant moments o'er
  And everlasting joy when Time shall be no more."

A watchmaker named Adams, who practised his craft many years ago in Church Street, Hackney, was fond of putting scraps of poetry in the outer case of watches sent him for repair. One of his effusions follow :

" To-morrow ! yes, to-morrow ! you'll repent
  A train of years in vice and folly spent.
  To-morrow comes—no penitential sorrow
  Appears therein, for still it is to-morrow ;
  At length to-morrow such a habit gains
  That you'll forget the time that Heaven ordains ;
  And you'll believe that day too soon will be
  When more to-morrows you're denied to see."

Another old engraved specimen contained this verse:

> "Content thy selfe withe thyne estat,
> And sende no poore wight from thy gate;
> For why, this councell I thee give,
> To learne to dye, and dye to lyve."

The following lines by Pope, occurring in his Epistle to the Earl of Oxford, have been used in this way:

> "Absent or dead
> Still let a friend be
> Dear. The Absent claims
> a sigh, the dead a
> tear.
> May
> Angels guard
> The friend I
> love."

Milman's poems have furnished a verse for this purpose:

> "It matters little at what hour o' the day
> The righteous fall asleep; death cannot come
> To him untimely who is fit to die.
> The less of this cold world, the more of heaven;
> The briefer life, the earlier immortality."

Various other examples of watch-case verses follow:

THE WATCH'S MOMENTS.

> "See how the moments pass,
> How swift they fly away!

In the instructive glass
Behold thy life's decay.
Oh ! waste not then thy prime
In sin's pernicious road ;
Redeem thy misspent time,
Acquaint thyself with God.
So when thy pulse shall cease
Its throbbing transient play,
The soul to realms of bliss
May wing its joyful way."

" Deign, lady fair, this watch to wear,
To mark how moments fly ;
For none a moment have to spare,
Who in a moment die."

To a Lady with the present of a Watch.

" With me while present, may thy lovely eyes,
Be never turned upon this golden toy ;
Think every pleasing hour too swiftly flies,
And measure time by joy succeeding joy.
But when the cares that interrupt our bliss,
To me not always will thy sight allow,
Then oft with fond impatience look on this,
Then every minute count—as I do now."

" Time is thou hast, employ the portion small ;
Time past is gone, thou canst not it recall ;
Time future is not, and may never be ;
Time present is the only time for thee."

" Watch against evil thoughts
Watch against idle words ;

Watch against sinful ways;
Watch against wicked actions.
What I say unto you I say unto all, Watch."

The following lines have a sand-glass engraved between the first four and the last four lines:

" Mark the rapid motion
    Of this timepiece ; hear it say,
Man, attend to thy salvation ;
    Time does quickly pass away.
Why, heedless of the warning
    Which my tinkling sound doth give,
Do forget, vain frame adorning,
    Man·thou art not born to live?"

On a sun-dial the following verse has been found engraved:

" Once at a potent leader's voice it stayed ;
Once it went back when a good monarch prayed ;
Mortals ! howe'er ye grieve, howe'er deplore,
The flying shadow shall return no more."

This was found under an hour-glass in a grotto near water :

" This babbling stream not uninstructive flows,
    Nor idly loiters to its destined main ;
Each flower it feeds that on its margin grows,
    Now bids thee blush, whose days are spent in vain.

Nor void of moral, though unheeded glides
    Time's current, stealing on with silent haste ;
For lo ! each falling sand *his* folly chides,
    Who lets one precious moment run to waste. "

PROSE POEMS.

EVERAL pages of this kind appeared at the end of an early volume of " Cornhill Magazine," of which this is the beginning :

To Correspondents.

" 'Tis in the middle of the night; and as with weary hand we write, ' Here endeth C. M. volume seven,' we turn our grateful eyes to heaven. The fainting soul, oppressèd long, expands and blossoms into song; but why 'twere difficult to state, for here commenceth volume eight.

" And ah ! what mischiefs him environ who claps the editorial tiar on ! 'Tis but a paper thing, no doubt; but those who don it soon find out the weight of lead— ah me, how weary !—one little foolscap sheet may carry. Pleasing, we hear, to gods and man was Mr. William Gladstone when he calmed the paper duty fuss ; but oh, 'twas very hard on Us. Before he took the impost off, one gentleman was found enough (he *was* Herculean, but still !—) to bear the letters from Cornhill : two men are needed now, and these are clearly going at the knees. Yet happy hearts had we to-day if one in fifteen hundred, say, of all the packets, white and blue, which we diurnally go through, yielded an ounce of sterling brains, or ought but headache for our pains. Ah, could the Correspondent see the Editor in his misery, no more injurious ink he'd shed, but tears of sympathy instead.

What is this tale of straws and bricks? A hen with
fifty thousand chicks clapt in Sahara's sandy plain to
peck the wilderness for grain—in that unhappy fowl is
seen the despot of a magazine. Only one difference
we find; but that is most important, mind. Instinct
compels *her* patient beak; ours—in all modesty we
speak—is kept by CONSCIENCE (sternly chaste) pegging
the literary waste. Our barns are stored, our garners
—well, the stock in them's considerable; yet when
we're to the desert brought, again comes back the welcome thought that somewhere in its depths may hide
one little seed, which, multiplied in our half-acre on
Cornhill, might all the land with gladness fill. Experi-
ence then no more we heed; but, though we seldom
find the seed, we read, and read, and read, and read."
&c. &c.

This is also an instance of this hidden verse in
the beginning of one of Macaulay's letters to his
sister Hannah:

"MY DARLING,—Why am I such a fool as to write to
a gipsy at Liverpool, who fancies that none is so good
as she if she sends one letter for my three? A lazy
chit, whose fingers tire in penning a page in reply to a
quire! There, miss, you read all the first sentence of
my epistle, and never knew that you were reading
verse."

When Mr. Coventry Patmore's "Angel in the
House" was first published, the "Athenæum"
furnished the following unique criticism:

"The gentle reader we apprise, That this new Angel

in the House Contains a tale not very wise, About a
person and a spouse. The author, gentle as a lamb,
Has managèd his rhymes to fit, And haply fancies
he has writ Another 'In Memoriam.' How his intended
gathered flowers, And took her tea and after sung, Is
told in style somewhat like ours, For delectation of the
young. But, reader, lest you say we quiz The poet's
record of his she, Some little pictures you shall see,
Not in our language but in his :

> ' While thus I grieved and kissed her glove,
>   My man brought in her note to say
> Papa had bid her send his love,
>   And hoped I dine with them next day ;
> They had learned and practised Purcell's glee,
>   To sing it by to-morrow night :
> The postscript was—her sisters and she
> Inclosed some violets blue and white.
>
>   .   .   .   .   .
>
> ' Restless and sick of long exile,
>   From those sweet friends I rode, to see
> The church repairs, and after a while
>   Waylaying the Dean, was asked to tea.
> They introduced the Cousin Fred
>   I'd heard of, Honor's favourite ; grave,
> Dark, handsome, bluff, but gently bred,
>   And with an air of the salt wave.'

Fear not this saline Cousin Fred ; He gives no tragic
mischief birth ; There are no tears for you to shed,
Unless they may be tears of mirth. From ball to bed,
from field to farm, The tale flows nicely purling on ;
With much conceit there is no harm, In the love-legend
here begun. The rest will come another day, If public

sympathy allows; And this is all we have to say About
the 'Angel in the House.'"

THE PRINTER.

"The printer-man had just set up a 'stickful' of
brevier, filled with italic, fractions, signs, and other things
most queer; the type he lifted from the stick, nor dreamt
of coming woes, when lo! a wretched wasp thought fit to
sting him on the nose: the printer-man the type let fall,
as quick as quick could be, and gently murmured a
naughty word beginning with a D."   .

MY LOVE.

"I seen her out a-walking in her habit de la rue, and
it ain't no use a-talking, but she's pumpkins and a few.
She glides along in glory like a duck upon a lake, and
I'd be all love and duty, if I only were her drake!"

THE SOLO.

"He drew his breath with a gasping sob, with a
quivering voice he sang, but his voice leaked out and
could not drown the accompanist's clamorous bang.   He
lost his pitch on the middle A, he faltered on the lower
D, and foundered at length like a battered wreck adrift
on the wild high C."

PONY LOST.

On Feb. 21st, 1822, this devil bade me adieu.

"Lost, stolen, or astray, not the least doubt but run
away, a mare pony that is all bay,—if I judge pretty
nigh, it is about eleven hands high; full tail and mane,
a pretty head and frame; cut on both shoulders by the
collar, not being soft nor hollow; it is about five years
old, which may be easily told; for spirit and for speed,
the devil cannot her exceed."

An excellent specimen of this kind of literary work is to be found in J. Russell Lowell's "Fable for Critics," of which the title-page and preface are written in this fashion, and there is here given an extract from the latter :

"Having scrawled at full gallop (as far as that goes) in a style that is neither good verse nor bad prose, and being a person whom nobody knows, some people will say I am rather more free with my readers than it is becoming to be, that I seem to expect them to wait on my leisure in following wherever I wander at pleasure,— that, in short, I take more than a young author's lawful ease, and laugh in a queer way so like Mephistopheles, that the public will doubt, as they grope through my rhythm, if in truth I am making fun *at* them or *with* them.

"So the excellent Public is hereby assured that the sale of my book is already secured. For there is not a poet throughout the whole land, but will purchase a copy or two out of hand, in the fond expectation of being amused in it, by seeing his betters cut up and abused in it. Now, I find, by a pretty exact calculation, there are something like ten thousand bards in the nation, of that special variety whom the Review and Magazine critics call *lofty* and *true,* and about thirty thousand (*this* tribe is increasing) of the kinds who are termed *full of promise* and *pleasing.* The public will see by a glance at this schedule, that they cannot expect me to be over-sedulous about courting *them,* since it seems I have got enough fuel made sure of for boiling my pot.

"As for such of our poets as find not their names mentioned once in my pages, with praises or blames, let them send in their cards, without further delay, to my friend G. P. Putnam, Esquire, in Broadway, where a list will be kept with the strictest regard to the day and the hour of receiving the card. Then, taking them up as I chance to have time (that is, if their names can be twisted in rhyme), I will honestly give each his proper position, at the rate of one author to each new edition. Thus, a premium is offered sufficiently high (as the Magazines say when they tell their best lie) to induce bards to club their resources and buy the balance of every edition, until they have all of them fairly been run through the mill." &c. &c.

That which is considered, however, one of the best of Prose Poems is the following, which appeared originally in *Fraser's Magazine*, and will also be found in Maclise and Maginn's "Gallery of Illustrious Literary Characters,"* being part of the introductory portion of a notice of the late Earl of Beaconsfield, then Mr. Disraeli, and known at the time as an aspirant to literary and political fame:

"O Reader dear! do pray look here, and you will spy the curly hair, and forehead fair, and nose so high, and gleaming eye, of Benjamin D'Is-ra-e-li, the wondrous boy who wrote *Alroy* in rhyme and prose, only to show how long ago victorious Judah's lion-banner rose. In an earlier day he wrote *Vivian Grey*—a smart

* London : Chatto & Windus.

enough story, we must say, until he took his hero abroad,
and trundled him over the German road; and taught
him there not to drink beer, and swallow schnapps, and
pull mädschen's caps, and smoke the cigar and the meer-
sham true, in alehouse and lusthaus all Fatherland
through, until all was blue, but talk secondhand that
which, at the first, was never many degrees from the
worst,—namely, German cant and High Dutch senti-
mentality, maudlin metaphysics, and rubbishing reality.
But those who would find how Vivian wined with the
Marchioness of Puddledock, and other great grandees
of the kind, and how he talked æsthetic, and waxed
eloquent and pathetic, and kissed his Italian puppies of
the greyhound breed, they have only to read—if the
work be still alive—Vivian Grey, in volumes five.

"As for his tentative upon the *Representative*, which
he and John Murray got up in a very great hurry, we
shall say nothing at all, either great or small; and all
the wars that thence ensued, and the Moravian's
deadly feud; nor much of that fine book, which is called
the 'Young Duke,' with his slippers of velvet blue, with
clasps of snowy-white hue, made out of the pearl's mother,
or some equally fine thing or other; and 'Fleming'
(*Contarini*), which will cost ye but a guinea; and 'Gallo-
mania' (get through it, can you?) in which he made
war on (assisted by a whiskered baron—his name was
Von Haber, whose Germanical jabber, Master Ben,
with ready pen, put into English smart and jinglish),
King Philippe and his court; and many other great
works of the same sort—why, we leave them to the
reader to peruse; that is to say, if he should choose.

"He lately stood for Wycombe, but there Colonel

Grey did lick him, he being parcel Tory and parcel Radical—which is what in general mad we call ; and the latest affair of his we chanced to see, is 'What is he?' a question which, by this time, we have somewhat answered in this our pedestrian rhyme. As for the rest, —but writing rhyme is, after all, a pest; and therefore "——

MISCELLANEOUS ODDS AND ENDS.

SOME years ago *Punch* gave "revised versions" of a few of the old popular songs, and, referring to the one we have chosen as a specimen, says that "its simplicity, its truthfulness, and, above all, its high moral, have recommended it to him for selection. It is well known to the million—of whose singing, indeed, it forms a part. Perhaps it will be recognised ; perhaps not."

A POLISHED POEM.

Air.—"If I had a donkey vot vouldn't go,
Do you think I'd wallop," &c.

" Had I an ass averse to speed,
Deem'st thou I'd strike him? No, indeed !
Mark me, I'd try persuasion's art,
For cruelty offends my heart :
Had all resembled me, I ween,
Martin, thy law had needless been
Of speechless brutes from blows to screen
            ·   The poor head ;
For had I an ass averse to speed

I ne'er would strike him, no, indeed!
I'd give him hay, and cry, ' Proceed,'
   And 'Go on, Edward!'

Why speak I thus?   This very morn,
I saw that cruel William Burn,
Whilst crying 'Greens' upon his course,
Assail his ass with all his force;
He smote him o'er the head and thighs,
Till tears bedimmed the creature's eyes!
Oh! 'twas too much, my blood 'gan rise
   And I exclaimed,
    ' Had I an,' &c.

Burn turn'd and cried, with scornful eye,
' Perchance thou'rt one of Martin's fry,
And seek'st occasion base to take,
The vile informer's gain to make.'
Word of denial though I spoke,
Full on my brow his fury broke,
And thus, while I return'd the stroke,
   I exclaimed,
    ' Had I an,' &c.

To us, infringing thus the peace,
Approach'd his guardians—the police;
And, like inevitable Fate,
Bore us to where stern Justice sate;
Her minister the tale I told;
And to support my word, made bold
To crave he would the ass behold:
    ' For,' I declared,
    ' Had I an,' &c.

They called the creature into court
Where, sooth to say, he made some sport,
With ears erect, and parted jaws,
As though he strove to plead his cause :
I gained the palm of feelings kind ;
The ass was righted ; William fined.
For Justice, one with me in mind,
                    Exclaimed, by her Minister,
                    ' Had I an,' &c.

Cried William to his judge, ' 'Tis hard
(Think not the fine that I regard),
But things have reached a goodly pass—
One may not beat a stubborn ass !'
Nought spoke the judge, but closed his book ;
So William thence the creature took,
Eyeing me—ah ! with what a look,
          As gently whispering in his ear, I said,
          ' William, had I an,' &c."

CUMULATIVE PARODYING.

There was a young damsel ; oh, bless her,
It cost very little to dress her ;
     She was sweet as a rose
     In her everyday clothes,
But had no young man to caress her.
                    —*Meridien Recorder.*

There was a young turkey ; oh, bless her :
It cost very little to dress her ;
     Some dry bread and thyme,
     About Thanksgiving time,
And they ate the last bit from the dresser.
                    —*American Punch.*

A newspaper poet ; oh, dang him !
And pelt him and club him and bang him !
 He kept writing away,
 Till the people one day
Rose up and proceeded to hang him.
      —*Detroit Free Press.*

Blank Verse in Rhyme.

(A nocturnal sketch.)]

" Even is come ; and from the dark Park, hark
 The signal of the setting sun—one gun !
 And six is sounding from the chime, prime time
 To go and see the Drury-lane Dane slain,—
 Or hear Othello's jealous doubt spout out,—
 Or Macbeth raving at that shade-made blade,
 Denying to his frantic clutch much touch ;
 Or else to see Ducrow with wide stride ride
 Four horses as no other man can span ;
 Or in the small Olympic pit, sit split
 Laughing at Liston, while you quiz his phiz.

 Anon night comes, and with her wings brings things
 Such as, with his poetic tongue, Young sung;
 The gas up-blazes with its bright white light,
 And paralytic watchmen prowl, howl, growl,
 About the streets, and take up Pall Mall Sal,
 Who hastening to her nightly jobs, robs fobs.

 Now thieves to enter for your cash, smash, crash,
 Past drowsy Charley, in a deep sleep, creep,
 But frightened by Policeman B 3, flee,
 And while they're going whisper low, ' No go !'
 Now puss, while folks are in their beds, treads leads,
 And sleepers waking, grumble—' Drat that cat !'
 Who in the gutter caterwauls, squalls, mauls
 Some feline foe, and screams in shrill ill-will.

Now Bulls of Bashan, of a prize-size, rise
In childish dreams, and with a roar gore poor
Georgey, or Charles, or Billy, willy-nilly ;
But nursemaid in a nightmare rest, chest-pressed,
Dreameth of one of her old flames, James Games,
And that she hears—what faith is man's !—Ann's banns
And his, from Reverend Mr. Rice, twice, thrice ;
White ribbons flourish, and a stout shout out,
That upward goes, shows Rose knows those bows' woes !"
—Thomas Hood.

The following excellent specimen of mono-syllabic verse comes from an old play in the Garrick Collection:

SONG.

" Let us sip, and let it slip,
    And go which way it will a ;
Let us trip, and let us skip,
    And let us drink our fill a.

Take the cup, and drink all up,
    Give me the can to fill a ;
Every sup, and every cup,
    Hold here and my good will a.

Gossip mine and gossip thine,
    Now let us gossip still a ;
Here is good wine, this ale is fine,
    Now drink of which you will a.

Round about, till all be out,
    I pray you let us swill a ;
This jolly grout is jolly and stout,
    I pray you stout it still a.

Let us laugh and let us quaff,
  Good drinkers think none ill a ;
Here is your bag, here is your staffe,
  Be packing to the mill a."

ELESSDÉ.

" In a certain fair island, for commerce renown'd,
  Whose fleets sailed in every sea,
A set of fanatics, men say, there was found,
Who set up an island and worship around,
  And called it by name Elessdé.

Many heads had the monster, and tails not a few,
  Of divers rare metals was he ;
And temples they built him right goodly to view,
Where oft they would meet, and, like idolists true,
  Pay their vows to the great Elessdé.

Moreover, at times would their frenzy attain
  ('Twas nought less) to so high a degree,
That his soul-blinded votaries did not complain,
But e'en laid down their lives his false favour to gain—
  So great was thy power, Elessdé.

As for morals, this somewhat unscrupulous race
  Were lax enough, 'twixt you and me ;
Men would poison their friends with professional grace,
And of the fell deed leave behind ne'er a trace,
  For the sake of the fiend, Elessdé.

Then forgery flourished, and rampant and rife
  Was each form of diablerie ;
While the midnight assassin, with mallet and knife,

Would steal on his victim and rob him of life,
And all for thy love, Elessdé.

There were giants of crime on the earth in that day,
The like of which we may not see :
Although, peradventure, some sceptic will say
There be those even now who acknowledge the sway
Of the god of the world—£ *s. d.*"

EARTH.

"What is earth, Sexton ?—A place to dig graves.
What is earth, Rich man ?—A place to work slaves.
What is earth, Greybeard ?—A place to grow old.
What is earth, Miser ?—A place to dig gold.
What is earth, Schoolboy?—A place for my play.
What is earth, Maiden ?—A place to be gay.
What is earth, Seamstress ?—A place where I weep.
What is earth, Sluggard ?—A good place to sleep.
What is earth, Soldier ?—A place for a battle.
What is earth, Herdsman ?—A place to raise cattle.
What is earth, Widow ?—A place of true sorrow.
What is earth, Tradesman ?—I'll tell you to-morrow.
What is earth, Sick man ?—'Tis nothing to me.
What is earth, Sailor?—My home is the sea.
What is earth, Statesman ?—A place to win fame.
What is earth, Author ?—I'll write there my name.
What is earth, Monarch ?—For my realm it is given.
What is earth, Christian ?—The gateway of heaven."

INDEX.

*Printed by Ballantyne, Hanson & Co.
Edinburgh and London.*

EXTRACTS FROM NOTICES

OF

"*LITERARY FRIVOLITIES, FANCIES, FOLLIES, AND FROLICS.*"

(Uniform with the present volume, post 8vo, cloth limp, 2s 6d.)

"THIS is a new volume of the popular Mayfair Library, and it well deserves its place. In such a book selection and arrangement are everything. . . . Mr. Dobson really knows what to choose and what to reject; he has also a feeling for good arrangement, and has made a most attractive volume. . . . For an odd half-hour or for a long journey we could hardly imagine anything better, and we trust the book may find the encouragement it so well deserves."—*British Quarterly Review.*

"'Literary Frivolities' is an absolutely delightful companion for an unoccupied half-hour. It is a book which may with equal pleasure be read all through or dipped into at any point, and the collection of literary triflings it supplies is admirably ample."—*Gentleman's Magazine.*

"This is a pleasant and amusing little volume. It contains a great deal o curious information, and shows a very creditable amount of research. . . . We may end as we began, by commending 'Literary Frivolities' as a capital book of its sort."—*Athenæum.*

"This latest volume of the bright little 'Mayfair Library' is an entertaining contribution to the literature of 'inert hours,' and will sufficiently initiate its readers into all the mysteries of bouts-rimés, palindromes, lipograms, centones and figurate poems."—*Notes and Queries.*

"A more delightful little work it has seldom been our lot to take in hand. Mr. Dobson has made a study of all the eccentricities and frivolities which have from time to time been perpetrated by writers in prose and verse. . . . Mr. Dobson had gone into his work in a catholic spirit, and has done it with great neatness and ability. It would be difficult to commend the book too highly. It is a volume alike for holiday purposes, and for other purposes more serious in connection with literature."—*Scotsman.*

"Mr. Dobson has done his work well. . . . The book is very interesting and entertaining, and has a still higher claim to our regard as a curious chapter in the history of literature."—*Examiner.*

"Not a few of the pages will raise a hearty laugh, and this fact alone disposes us to regard the book with marked favour. A good index has not been forgotten, and the volume in all ways reflects high credit on its author."—*Brief.*

"This is a queer collection of interesting nothings, a record of some of the literary playthings wherewith men have sought at one time and another to beguile the road towards the darkness. Here are quips and cranks, strange forms of prose and verse ; monstrosities of rhythms. It is all very interesting, and shows a heavy amount of research on the part of the compiler." —*Vanity Fair.*

"Great fun is shown in almost every page of ' Literary Frivolities.' . . . The ' Mayfair Library ' will do well if it gives us many books like Mr. Dobson's."
—*Graphic.*

"It is quite certain that there have been thousands of not only intelligent, but grave and learned persons who have taken pride as well as pleasure in the accomplishment of such exploits, and that there are tens of thousands who will be greatly entertained, if not roused to emulation, by the pretty little volume consecrated to the commemoration and to illustrative samples of those exploits. . . . It is provided with an index, a very useful addition, and it is undoubtedly a bright, amusing, and not altogether uninstructive publication."
—*Illustrated London News.*

"Mr. Dobson deserves credit for the pains he has taken."—*Spectator.*

"A miscellaneous and highly amusing collection of literary curiosities."—*Bookseller.*

"An amusing volume. . . . An account of a great many of those curious puzzles and tasks in which the literary mind delights."—*Teacher.*

"A collection, a most exhaustive one, of the vagaries indulged in from remote ages down to the present day by literary triflers."—*Whitehall Review.*

"A very entertaining little book. . . . Exceedingly interesting, and may be heartily recommended."—*Nottingham Guardian.*

"A capital little book. . . . A cheap and neat volume which no editor or printer should be without."—*Printing Times and Lithographer.*

"One of the most quaintly amusing books we have seen for a long time."
—*Edinburgh Evening Express.*

"For a man or woman endowed with literary tastes, and who, for want of regular work to do, sometimes longs for new methods of ' killing time,' this collection of frivolities and oddities might prove a fruitful source of amusement. Its author is a scholarly and well-read man ; and in preparing this book he must have put himself to an infinitude of pains."—*Edinburgh Daily Review.*

"The little volume is pleasantly and learnedly written."—*One and All.*

CHATTO AND WINDUS, PICCADILLY, W.